TRESPASS

Other books by the author:

Underwater (1974 and 2014)

Bailey (2011)

Rematch (2021)

Family Money (2022)

TRESPASS

a novel

JOAN HAWKINS

Landon Books
NEW YORK

First Published by

Landon Books, New York, 2013
First Electronic Edition by
Landon Books, New York, 2013

www.JoanHawkins.net

ISBN 978-0-9837348-3-3

Book and cover design by www.Cyberscribe.eu

TRESPASS

1

Helen Reed, a wealthy widow, was dying. Because the cancer could be a savage beast chewing her spine, she'd hired herself a tamer. Her daughter Barbara Stone had learned over the telephone, that David Sweeney, Helen's wonderful masseur, had accepted her offer to live in the house. The proof of his commitment to help her live until she died were the drums that he'd carried up to the attic rooms.

Bright, red beautiful drums, Barbara Stone told her husband at supper. He'd toted cymbals too.

"You say the punk has moved into Helen's house?" Jake Stone poured whiskey and turned his calm face to his wife. "He's in her house? Are you serious, Barbara? Is she Christy?" Jake Stone looked at his daughter.

Chewing noisily, Christine Stone, the only child of her parents, appeared not to hear her father's question.

"Our daughter's in a feeding frenzy and doesn't know we're here."

With a courteous little bow, Jake Stone placed a drink in his wife's hand, then rapped the table in front of Christy's plate.

"The deadly parasite has bored deep into his prey. You've got to look sharp this summer, kid. Be the family spy."

Christy looked up from her plate. "A parasite? Are you talking about grandma's cancer?"

"Another kind of cancer, darling. An immoral, scheming, thieving kind – you know." Cheerfully, he inquired into the whereabouts of her mind when, night after night, her parents discussed the danger presented to the family by this absurd young man from Timbuktu – this damned David Sweeney.

"I'm just eating, dad."

"Gorging!" He pointed to her loaded plate. "For weeks now you've sat here while your mother and I have argued over the intentions of this supposed masseur and yet you say that you don't know who is being described by the word 'parasite?'"

"I don't."

"Where are you going mentally all these nights?"

"I don't remember."

"Obviously you remember what you were thinking ten minutes ago." His sardonic smile greeted the girl's shy gaze.

In her imagination, as the nightly discussion raged, Christy was faint from the force of David Sweeney. Chewing her mother's delicious dinners, wetness poured onto her underpants and her legs ached with desire. Since spring, when her grandmother began to report the extraordinary ability of an intense young man to massage away the dreadful pain in her back, David Sweeney had been the most prized mental possession of Christine Stone – her most secret.

Formerly a child fiercely taken up with competitions in school, now her victories came only from the push of her will – her enthusiasm asleep until supper time.

Her mother's cooking was the best! The pastas, the meats, the vegetables! Oh, god, she ate in ecstasy while David Sweeney, the subject of her parents' argument, filled her dreaming mind. He was a musician who, to her father's disgust, wore his black hair back in a ponytail. He wrote songs, played the drums and was currently in exile from the music scene.

To write wonderful songs, her mother was certain.

To survive as a failure, Christy's father had no doubt.

In her fantasy Christy was the young musician's protégé because her talent was amazing. Even while her father waited for an answer to his question – his eyes holding steady on her own – her inward eye saw drumsticks taken from her hands as David Sweeney pulled her up and crushed her against his chest.

"Here's your idiotic expression again. Now, Christy, tell me what's on your mind."

"I've been playing the drums in school, dad. I'm going to be a drummer."

11

"Don't be ridiculous. Drumming isn't anything."

Christy was as surprised as her father by her spontaneous ambition. His comfortable confidence, for the first time resented, hardened her words to decree. She announced that in the fall when she returned to school, she would quit gymnastics and take up the drums.

"Drummers are the mud men of music. No brains, no culture. Every last one of them is a scoundrel. Tomorrow, when you meet this masseur; I want your first look at him to be through my eyes. You must observe him as the enemy of our family and be our spy."

Barbara Stone slid more veal on her daughter's plate, telling her to ignore her father's cynicism and his absurd request.

"You can't help but be attracted to this young man no matter what you're told to think. So celebrate the summer, darling. Be happy. Be passionate."

Blushing again, this time Christy was embarrassed and confused by the extravagance and sadness of her mother's exhortation. She concentrated on the delicious veal while her parents argued – her father disliked her mother's sentimentality while she scorned his peasant's greed.

In the fridge for two days, the cutlets had been soaking up the tuna sauce and the taste and texture of the meat raised her skin in goosebumps, as, chewing slowly, she lifted more meat off the platter.

"Hold on, now. You'll be sick."

Frightened by her father's alarm, Christy glanced at

her mother, who was drinking, not eating, and momentarily absorbed in a gloomy mood.

"Early man was a skinny little thing, you know. Ate just a tad of meat because it was so difficult to kill an animal. However, quantities of nuts and berries went down his throat. Bushels of fruit." The teasing in Jake Stone's voice turned sharp.

"You won't burn fat beating a stretched cow hide."

"Why should I?"

"Stuffing yourself the way you have tonight, you'll be obese in a week if you stop your gymnastics for drumming. You've already put on a few pounds."

"No way!"

"Let's have a look at you."

As Christy cleared the table and washed the dishes she was completely confident that her father would approve of her appearance. It was nothing new for him to rumble about her appetite or even mandate a diet to achieve her perfect weight, but always she'd felt excited, as though his keen eyes were the spotlights on her romantic life.

Feelings of modesty and dignity, the qualities he most admired, tingled along her spine and over her shoulders as she vigorously scoured a frying pan.

"Your daughter's become heavy overnight, Barbara."

"Christy's growing up."

"She's gotten fat."

Drying her hands on her jeans, Christy faced her parents with a strained smile.

"Fat or growing up, what do you say, folks?"

In the boom of their dissent, Christy laughed at being two things at once. Side by side on their march through life, they were both so solid. In her mind she ran between their contrary confidences like a polite servant.

"She'll be fifteen in a month, Jake." Hopping up from the table, Barbara Stone kissed her dismayed daughter and gave her behind a humorous pat. "She's a blooming young woman."

"Yeah, dad." Grinning, Christy assumed her usual stance of cheerful confrontation with her adored father. Feet wide, knees bent, she could have been catching a baseball he'd thrown. But replacing the friendly challenge she was used to seeing in his eyes there was unease. His stern glance at her breasts made her feel ugly and then disloyal.

"I'm just so hungry these days, dad."

"So what?"

"Right now I could eat pizza – two slices with peppers, mushrooms and extra cheese." Christy crossed her arms over her breasts and twirled on her toes. But instead of invoking the admired, attractive child of her father's approbation, she felt idiotic and unrefined.

"You've been taught to curb your hunger."

Her father, rather proud of his own physique, was of the opinion that going through the day on the hungry side made the mind and body tough and strong.

"I'll try not to eat so much, dad."

"You'll try?"

"I only remember not to eat when I'm stuffed. I can't help it," she appealed to her mother who laughed and repeated that she was a blooming young woman.

Christy still looked like a child to him, Jake Stone chided his wife. A greedy one no doubt, but still a child.

"Greedy?" Christy whispered.

"You're eating like a beast."

"Then I am a beast," she challenged him with frightened eyes. "All human beings are – but I'm not fat! I'm a teenager. America's finest."

Smiling, blushing, her head held high, but feet chaotic, Christy rushed, laughing, from the kitchen and down the hall to her room.

2

In a rush of mortification, Christy danced around her room. Unbelievable her father's anger, real this time, not teasing, and her own anger flying from her mouth. He'd taken bread from her hand before, cut her off candy, but in a friendly and admiring way. Tonight, however, he'd disliked her when she'd tried to be charming, and sassing him back had made him unhappy.

Qué pasa?

The window of her room looked out on the courtyard. At night it became a mirror where dancing, posing, whatever, she admired her image with grateful excitement.

Was she fat?

Certainly her legs were thin, as were her arms and torso. Was her ass? Looking over her shoulder, from the corner of her eye, Christy stared at the image of her behind and could not discover with her cruel hand the extra flesh of her father's accusation.

Except her breasts. Beneath her clothes it was like harboring the sweetest pets, their warmth and movement. Her former boy's chest had been a shield between her body and emotion, a barrier to exciting realms. But her father's drawing attention to her had been awful – so confusing and grim. His hard eyes, his hard voice saying the word "fat."

Squatting, Christy rapped the windowsill with both hands. The steady beat resounded like gunshots in the courtyard. Whap, whap, whap, whap! Fat or blooming, hard and fast as she could hit, her flying hands sought a path.

"Christine Stone, child of scorn, where were you when your mother was born?"

"Scorn? You mean I'm fat?" Christy twisted to see her butt in the black glass of the window while her mother perched on the end of the bed, pulling her own feet high on her thighs. The ice in her drink tinkled gaily as she balanced the full glass on her head to show Christy with a wink that her back was as straight as Buddha's.

"Dad thinks I'm fat – oh god!"

"That's good yoga." Barbara Stone admired her daughter's flourishing figure. "In your father's mind you're still ten years old. Your bloom on a child *would* be audacious."

"Audacious? I speak English, man!"

"Bold."

"Audacious? Bold? But is it cellulose?" Christy faced her mother in a panic. "I *am* fat!"

"Not on your life! You're beautifully thin. Trust me!"

"Why doesn't dad notice? I mean," Christy blushed.

"It's so obvious."

"He's terribly worried about the firm. All the partners have stopped taking their share of the profits."

"Why?"

"They've got to keep up with the changing times – but haven't."

Mother and daughter shared a sudden drift of mind at the unimaginable circumstance of financial danger. The lavish income Jake Stone provided with unspoken chivalry had blinded his dependents to the struggle its earning entailed. They had come to believe, however politely, that their own pursuits were more valuable.

"Can't dad depend on grandma?"

"Yes, but when?"

"When?"

"When will mother go ahead and die?"

Christy stared in horror at the large cloth bag she'd been packing for a week. "I'll never, ever pack for Weston again."

"Hopefully not."

Unknowingly, Christy imitated her mother's expression of cheerful conspiracy while her heart pounded in fright.

"Every summer of my life I've gone to grandma's."

"To be a little Victorian girl. To be really a doll the way mother smothers you in dresses and frets about what you eat and how you sleep. God forbid you should swim over your head or walk to town or be even a speck in the gaze of some man. I know what a struggle it is to be even allowed out of bed in the morning. A tiny cough or circles under your eyes can keep you in pajamas until lunch. Hours in bed with the yellow window shades like evil eyes in the morning sun and becoming really sick with boredom. God, you're a saint to endure it."

Barbara Stone gulped down mouthfuls of her drink.

"Every summer not only do you step backwards into the Victorian age, but you convince mother that you're happy spending the summer with her. If it weren't for your great heart, you know, I wouldn't be getting mother's money. It should be your inheritance – yes, it should, Christy, for the boredom you've endured – the frightful boredom of mother's life."

"I won't have my birthday in the garden anymore. The arbor will be sold."

"The house, too."

"No more grapes," the girl lamented.

"No more mother."

"Poor grandma."

As the unimaginable event of her grandmother's permanent absence converted to the ending of Christy's cherished summer visits, she groaned with regret. But Barbara Stone, drinking, could only see her own thoughts and felt Christy's emotion to be polite, not passionate.

"You're a noble child – really, you are. No one but you could see any poetry in that tomb of a mind. Eat it, drink it, wear it is mother's notion of a well-spent life. And she's decided to indulge her taste for expensive Scotch. Did I tell you that she's putting in a swimming pool, because even if she's too ill to go to the beach she must have her daily swim? My god, to pour twenty thousand dollars into a hole in the ground when you're at death's door is a scandal. I mean, Christy darling, can we bury her in the pool?"

As though energy was truth, the strength of her mother's opinions always converted Christy to her view. Agreement was happiness, even while she remembered her grandmother's collection of bathing caps – the pastel yellows, pinks and blues – to match her many bathing suits, and the gentle variation of her mood from day to day.

"Grandma loves to swim so much."

"But the point is that dying is serious – not a last vulgar shopping spree."

Suddenly, Barbara Stone gave up the yoga-straightness of her back, and normal state of mind. It happened every night as she drank, but the mournful yearning in her eyes remained a mystery to Christy.

"You're in the Scotch zone, ma."

"You mean I'm drunk, you courteous girl. It's true I see the amber truth in everything, but I'm not intoxicated." She tossed her empty glass to Christy and propped her elbows on her knees. As she supported her head on her hands her position seemed too buoyant a frame for her gloom.

"If people like me didn't make things – what would mother spend her money on? She buys everything under the sun but she won't buy my paintings. Not any, not one, never, because I'm not famous. Because fame hasn't justified my rebellion, because, blah, blah, blah."

"Grandma doesn't understand why you paint so much, but I do." Christy pointed at one of her mother's paintings that hung above her desk.

"That's beautiful! I look at it all the time. You're good, ma."

"You could be my mother the way you keep me going."

"I just tell the truth. Someday the whole world will know what a great painter you are." Christy turned her eyes away from her mother's wistful gaze.

"Not even you, whom she adores, could make my mother appreciate my talent. But what do I care about myself? I'm just the genetic link from something worse to something better."

"I'm not better than you." As she did every night, Christy fought her mother's increasing sorrow. "You say that too much."

"I love watching the young boys and girls on the streets and everywhere. There's such a gay mutuality of affection and respect. Yesterday, in the park, I saw a young girl on a bench holding a boy in her arms. She bent and kissed him. Now, that never could have been me back in the old dark days, but any one of these wonderful girls that I watch could be you, darling."

In her drunken absorption, Barbara Stone mistook her daughter's embarrassment for shy pleasure.

"You're blushing! So it is wonderful, this new, free age. You're enjoying it."

"I don't fool around, ma. You know that."

"You were brought up to enjoy it." Barbara Stone continued her thought as if her daughter hadn't spoken. "Mother thought you'd never survive being raised like a boy – oh, god did she bitch about the football – but I've never seen a more beautiful body – so pure and uninhibited. You're androgynous like all the marvelous young women tennis players and when you meet the right fellow, you'll never be unhappy again."

The fear aroused by her father, that he could see the fantasy always spinning in her mind, again gripped the girl as she avoided her mother's mournful stare.

The vital musician with his force and glowing talent was her most cherished mental possession, as well as her guiltiest.

"Meet the right fellow? I'm going to be a drummer. I don't care about guys."

"The right man will love you the way you love yourself. You'll feel as charged and natural as if you were swimming, but you won't be swimming in the sea. You'll love his smell."

"Smell?" Christy giggled with torment.

"Like grass."

"Drinking makes you so sad." And dumb, Christy agonized. Every night her admirable mother got so dumb and gloomy.

"It's sad to be me."

"You have fun in the morning when you're painting. It looks like a sword fight." Lunging at an imaginary canvas Christy attempted to rouse her mother to the cheer and vigor of her sober personality. She quoted a review about her last show. "Some critic said you're exciting, ma."

"I'm rotten," she stared at her daughter with shame. "But, you're good – an improvement, mother says, and that's enough for me to have done in my life, isn't it? To have boosted you?"

Woefully staring, Barbara Stone was blotto as Christy unlocked her legs from the lotus position and pulled her to her feet. Pliable to lead, Christy felt she was returning a sweet, runaway child as she brought her mother to the parents' room.

"She's out, is she?" Jake Stone put down his book and took his wife from Christy's charge.

"What's the matter with her, dad?"

Competent, tender, the lawyer put his wife to bed while his daughter watched from the doorway.

"Ask your mother that at breakfast tomorrow and she won't know what you're talking about." Settled again in the handsome wing chair, Jake Stone reached for his book.

"She'll wake up hungry, make a good breakfast and be working in the back room all day long." Surprised by Christy's somber concern, he closed the book on his lap.

"Your mother works hard, has a drink too many and passes out. So what?"

"Why is she so stupid when she talks about romance? She sounds like a soap opera, like a fool. I hate it."

"That's liquor talking, darling. That mood always burns off by morning."

"If you could hear her, dad. She makes sex sound like paradise. When I meet the right man I'm going to be happy forever. That's pathetic. It is!" Christy frowned at her father's sweet smile. "Something awful is happening to mother."

"You're seeing the effect of liquor and worry — nothing more."

"You mean, grandma?"

"And money."

Christy lay across the bed and briefly held her mother's hand. "Liquor turns her into another person. It's awful."

"A person she'll never meet, my darling, because your mother cannot be drunk and sober at the same time."

"That's smart, dad, but you can't really know if she doesn't remember."

Having resisted his wife's bold desire for the past few weeks, Jake Stone rejected the traces of resentment in her morning manner. Her drunken determination to love him quite often pushed him to be rough and at breakfast he convinced himself that a whopping hangover was the cause of her chagrin.

"Your mother doesn't hide the way she feels." They both smiled at this understatement of Barbara Stone's volubility. "She sings in the morning with a tranquil mind, believe me."

"Just now, when she told me that the right man would make me happy forever, she looked so young when she said it – younger than me."

"Christy, darling, your mother doesn't remember this forlorn apparition of herself."

"Appa - what? Speak English, please."

Frowning, Jake pointed his finger.

"If you don't know that apparition means ghost then you're not reading enough. Have you packed your school reading list?"

"Only dead people have ghosts, right?"

"You really must get down to reading this summer, will you, Christy?"

Her father's alarm that she wasn't working hard enough to overcome her weak vocabulary stung Christy. What he was really highlighting was her potential vulnerability in the horrendous competition for college. This new train of thought buried her frail insight that drinking revived the person that her mother had once been.

"I always read the required number of books."

"Do you look up all the words you don't know and copy out the definitions?"

"Grandma and I always read on the porch after breakfast. I ask her."

"I wouldn't depend on Helen this summer. She's taking very strong drugs – you understand."

The sound of her grandmother's bracelets as she 'wrestled' with the newspaper, the stories causing her to hum or sigh, the smell of her powder and the boxwood hedge that enclosed the porch were anguished memories as Christy agreed with her father that it would be best to pack her dictionary and her jogging sneakers.

Even if the swimming pool were finished on schedule, its small size would prohibit any serious exercise and Christy should get into the swing of running – in the morning or evening – perhaps both times of day. There was no better way to keep her weight down.

"Grandma would forbid me to jog."

"What do you mean?"

"She doesn't approve of violent exercise for girls, especially in the heat. I'd never be able to swim as long as I do at the Club if she didn't play cards with her friends. When grandma's got a good hand, I could swim the Sound and back."

"Well, then, you can run when Helen's at the card table."

"I never do what grandma doesn't allow."

Jake challenged Christy's proclamation of obedience with friendly confidence. After her freewheeling winters she'd go crazy if she didn't bend the Weston rules.

"I do just what grandma does from morning 'til night."

"What, you mean you never ask for a sandwich instead of that heavy midday meal? You watch the soap operas and the game shows? You never refuse to put on a dress for dinner?"

"Never!"

"Come on, now! You're as independent as I am when you're living in this apartment."

"In Weston, I'm grandma's sweet, Victorian girl."

Because he believed that his daughter only tolerated the stifling summer life, Jake mistook Christy's sorrow for depression.

"You've been a wonderful sport over the years. If it weren't for your summer visits to Weston your mother and grandmother would live as strangers. I know you'd rather be with your friends."

"No, I wouldn't."

"Oh, stop it."

"I like –" her father's disbelief was daunting.

"I really don't mind spending two months of the year with grandma."

"You gallantly stick out three months, Christy. Give yourself credit. "But," he exhorted, "tomorrow begins your last tour of duty."

"It's grandma's last summer," the girl lamented. "The difference that the warm weather brings makes her so excited. Reading on the porch instead of inside, switching all her routes to the local roads, hearing the frogs and the crickets, eating fresh corn and tomatoes from the garden – and grapes."

In her reverie Christy forgot her father's disapproval of Helen Reed's frivolous life and happily chatted.

"Do you know that grandma can never drive over the

bay bridge without a shot of vodka from her flask. 'High adventure,' she calls it. Oh, god, grandma has such fun."

"Fun? What a word for it, Christy."

"For what?"

Helen Reed's passionate attention to petty pleasures, Jake Stone lectured with disgust, the fortune she lavished on a house with no books, on a body with no mind. How could a life devoted to killing time be described as fun?

"It couldn't be?"

Jake laughed gently as Christy watched him for a clue.

"Well, what do you think? Is your grandmother enjoying her life or is she merely staving off boredom?"

The girl's unease became fright. "She's bored, dad? Right? Am I right?"

"Are you?"

Thinking of her grandmother's infectious excitement as she cleared the hurdles of her day, her flask to her lips in merry celebration, her twinkling eyes, Christy tried to understand the deeper truth that was lodged so firmly in her father's intelligent mind. One eye closed, her mouth twisted, she peered at him as though catching a ball facing the sun.

"I'm wrong, right?"

"You're adorable." Jake leapt up and threw his arm around her shoulder. "You're a diplomat with a heart – a wonderful child."

Escorting her back to her bedroom, his counsel was imperative. She must not forget to pack her dictionary and her jogging shoes. Her weight gain was alarming but easy to undo. He looked forward to seeing her down to fighting trim by 4th July – her birthday.

"Can I depend on you, Christy?"

"You bet."

3

"Stop, stop! You must stop this drumming!"

Like every other morning, her disobedience again discovered, Christy shrieked to see her grandmother so gray in the doorway. Since their life together last summer, at some terrible point over the winter, the gentle colors of her body's weather had retreated before an endless cloudy day. No bursts or glints or sweeps of friendly sunshine escaped the pall, and, except when she talked, a bleak imposter was wearing the familiar silk dresses and nimble shoes.

"Why do you look so frightened? Have you committed a crime?" Her ironic eyes briefly acknowledged Christy's panic at her ugly deterioration, then rescued them with fiction. It was only the damn drums that kept drawing Christy from their tried and true routine.

"You've only made the old lady toil up three flights of stairs on a hot June morning. What's that to look so glum about?"

Taking guilty advantage of the noble diplomacy, Christy whispered that she couldn't resist them.

"Much too pretty to resist." The red metal sparkling in the sun hurt the widow's eyes.

"Come now! David's cleared all the leaves from the pool. Yellow leaves, Christy. Only the beginning of June and the grass is dying in this drought. We'd fry in the car if we had to drive to the club," she tugged Christy's sleeve. "But we've got a beautiful swimming pool right in our own back yard. You don't want to be drumming in this inferno. Down these dark stairs we go."

Christy bounded to her grandmother, but when she felt the distant touch of her fingers she stole her arm away and, lagging behind, ignored her heart breaking uncertainty on the stairs.

"My perfect pool!" cried the widow, trotting out into the yard. "A perfect shape! Honestly, Christy, I don't like all this drumming. It's unhealthy in this ghastly heat. Why do you do it?"

"I'm practicing, grandma."

"Practicing?" Helen Reed fondly teased. "Whatever for?"

"I'm going to be a drummer."

"You're not, my darling."

"I'm not?" Her grandmother was a good news prophet with her admiring eyes and serene assurance.

"It's my summer challenge to shake your mother's ideas out of your head. This year I thought I'd be too weak

– but who should appear but wonderful David Sweeney. No, my dear child, you are not going to be a drummer. Now, jump into your suit and have a good swim before lunch."

Joyful as her grandmother watched her, Christy performed her swimming strokes with style. When she saw her grandmother sleeping under the yellow umbrella she practiced her "forbidden tricks" – the acrobatics she'd learned over the winter. The stiff board sprang her high enough for somersaults but not for a double front flip, which she strained to execute while David Sweeney, unnoticed behind the yellow umbrella, stood watching.

Where was the girl coming from? Often he'd seen and admired her brave grace, but where did she get such drive? It was very likely impossible to work two somersaults into a dive off such a low board, but evidently, the girl would die trying. Whenever he showed her a drill on the drums she wouldn't quit until she got it down. Her excitement over his drumming was a real turn-on, but his advice and demonstrations could enrage her. "Fuck off," she'd shout, scaring him silly.

When Christy first asked him if he wanted to have an affair, nervousness enfeebled the thrill. Her will and stamina would have intimidated him at sixteen and now, a decade later, he'd jokingly refused to disappoint her. One night Christy woke him up.

"You'll hate me," he moaned as she climbed into his bed. But she was only stoical and sweetly sad. She covered the drops of blood on the sheet with his tee shirt and answered his concern with a headstand, her balance perilous while she laughed. Her sensuality was frank and joyful until it died during sex.

David ducked under the umbrella and sat down beside Helen Reed. The girl who played dead to his passion and this athlete of awesome force and will — what was the connection, he wondered. Feeling fear and tenderness in rapid succession, David watched the old woman wake in panic when Christy walloped into the water on her back. She became frantic as the girl darted out of the pool and stepped onto the diving board.

"Stop her, David. She'll kill herself."

Christy shook off his hand then groaned at her forgetfulness. Her ardent apology to her grandmother was undoubtedly sincere, although David knew the girl would be diving again when Helen Reed took her nap. For the past three weeks practicing on his drums, the continual apology after her disobedience never came stale from the girl. Always sorry, always drumming, Christy's behavior inclined David Sweeney to his employer's assertion that her teen-aged granddaughter still had the soul of a child.

"Swim gently, darling, while David brings out lunch."

In the water again, Christy grinned at Helen Reed as though moderation was her heart's delight.

"You look so pretty, darling! I love to watch you."

"I love this summer, grandma! It's the best!"

The girl's radiant smile as she performed a gentle

breaststroke included David Sweeney. The widow turned her head and looked sharply into his eyes.

"You don't mind this little crush of hers?"

"I like her very much."

"If you want to keep her away from your drums, you must lock your door. They're an attractive nuisance, you know."

"Christy's learning a lot, Helen."

"Don't all children yearn to be rock stars?"

Her intelligent eyes looking steadily at his, David felt a danger in too readily agreeing that Christy was emotionally much younger than the adolescent she appeared to be. In her sudden suspicious mood, Helen Reed could think he was reaching for an alibi.

"The kid's turning fifteen in a couple of days."

"What? You call my elegant granddaughter 'the kid?'"

"You call her elegant?" David mimicked her pique. "She hasn't combed her hair since she's been in your house and the way she eats! I can hear her chewing out in the kitchen. Elegant? Not yet, Helen!"

"Oh, her manners! That's the crime of her mother and her artistic pretentions. You'll see the child corrected as the summer goes along – but even if I were talking about her body, it's a little angel that you see stepping out of the pool."

The girl's nipples were so conspicuous under the thin material of her bathing suit that David suspected Helen Reed was trying again to expose his sexual interest in her granddaughter.

"For an angel she's sure packing on the pounds."

"The child looks so grim and gaunt when she comes to me after the winter. I welcome the arrival of her little tummy. It's my yearly contribution to her health – your contribution now, my good friend – I can't cook anymore. I hope there's lots of chicken salad for lunch."

"LUNCH!" A strap of her bathing suit slid down her arm as Christy came running. For an instant David stared hard at her lovely breasts then turned his head and grinned at his employer.

"I'll give you cute."

"Hurry, you must feed her."

Filling trays in the kitchen and carrying them out, the young man welcomed the protection of the old lady's illusion that her granddaughter was not yet mature enough to be involved in sex. A few nights before he'd asked Christy if she wasn't also relieved by her grandmother's naivety and her answer still troubled his pride.

The sick woman's body and her own were racing apart and Christy was a sad rider. The old days – when she'd been the good child in her grandmother's house – was a paradise that would never come again.

"No offense," she cuffed him – but he'd asked.

Jealous, he'd attacked her romanticism. Surely, she was happy when she was drumming. Her enthusiasm for music was inspiring and he'd written some of his best songs since she'd come to spend the summer in the Weston house. And what child wouldn't find the long, hot days of her grandmother's petty regime occasionally oppressive.

Her grandmother's rule was the best, Christy replied. It was the beautiful summer smells, the tomatoes and corn from the garden, reading fairy tales on the porch and Helen Reed's charming exaltation if every day went to plan.

Eagerly she trotted around in her summer silk dresses – that now hung on her. Oh, god, she was dying so quickly and she wouldn't admit to her pain. Shriveling up, she'd sweat and smile. Did she groan in her room alone with David? Urgently, Christy wanted to know, then was horrified at the stoicism that the young man described. Helen Reed's silent suffering made the house so lonely. Christy could feel the cold, cruel universe even when she was drumming. It was HORRIBLE!

David Sweeney scorned her melodrama. If the universe was dreadful then where did Helen's joy come from? Where did she get her marvelous capacity to work if she wasn't a child of the Divine Spirit?

"In the universe, life is possible, but not invited," was her cool reply. But life would stay as long as it could – and this summer Christy was happy, because her body was strong. For the time being, unlike her darling grandmother, she wasn't wracked with pain.

She must think him a charlatan then, a faker. If he wasn't a conduit of divine energy, then what did she make of him?

"My father thinks you're a fortune hunter."

Demanding to know her own opinion, David laughed when she smiled and replied that all she knew was what everyone else was thinking. Helen Reed said that his wonderful hands helped her more than drugs, and if she had to listen to his damn talk about the value of suffering and the reality of the afterlife, well, she didn't mind.

"Helen's got to know where she's going," David replied with such pleasant factuality that Christy shivered and grew shy.

The huge salary that Helen Reed paid him and the prospect of a legacy when she died was vital to the young man, but he adored her. As much as she was his guru who confirmed his belief in God, Helen Reed inspired him. The beauty of her voice, her eyes and gestures all indicated a sparkling idealism, but her values were worldly and her thoughts provincial. Accurately, she described herself as a 'funny little person,' who cared only for her house, her garden and her granddaughter. Her zest at upkeep was astonishing.

At twenty-five, in exile from the music scene but somewhat known, David Sweeney had never felt such pleasure at another's praise. The widow's cheerful assurance of his worth on the planet was so charming. He was going deeper with his playing and writing; for the first time in years he was out of bed in the morning with a sober and happy mind.

He loved his room in the vast, proper house and in his paid duties to Helen Reed, he could take care of a woman without his usual turmoil of pride. Her Victorian denial of the body made her unselfconscious. Tending and toting her like a child, her grateful proclamation that his massages drove out her pain complicated the world's suspicion that he was only after her fortune.

"Martinis — what a good idea."

"I have it every day, Helen." David Sweeney poured her drink from a silver shaker.

"You're a delightful young man." The widow smiled at him as she sipped. "How pretty the table looks. Was I asleep while you set it? Yes? Well, never mind. Didn't die anyway. I'd hate to die before I had my drinks. The chicken salad looks divine. And you've done something wonderful with the deviled eggs. Get Christy, David. My mouth is watering. Oh, my, what a wonderful lunch."

Helen Reed never ate a bite before she'd drunk three cocktails and even then her will to eat hardly prevailed against her nausea and fatigue, but her brave enthusiasm excited David and he fetched Christy as though inviting her to a feast.

The widow laughed at their antics beside the pool, the two trying to push each other in. The gay scene had been utterly unthinkable until a summer ago. Had she dreamed of a swimming pool in the backyard or just thought of it early one winter morning before she'd gotten out of bed to begin the day?

Carefully she'd visualized the yard in its winter desolation and then with a swimming pool of beautiful shape – befriended by the summer trees and grass. She'd hoped the contractor would discover an underground spring so that the water would be cool and sparkling even in the dog days, but instead she was paying a fortune for the electricity used by the cooling unit. She felt the coolness now in the drops of water sent through the air by Christy's whirling hair. Her knees bent, she was snapping her head up and back to shoot out the water.

"Puppies do that, Christy, not young girls."

"Do you think my hair will stay blonde, grandma?" Sitting down at the glass-topped table next to Helen Reed, Christy pulled a strand of her wet hair over her shoulder and studied it.

"You'll keep that lovely color for a good long time."

"Do you think that's wrong?"

"I loved my hair too."

"Were you a blonde?"

"My hair was as beautiful as yours is now – for years and years. I can show you a picture." The widow laughed at her granddaughter's unconscious dismay. "Oh, is it as ghastly as that? It's still thick, after all."

"You look beautiful! I love your hair. It is thick. You look like a lioness when you leave it out. You know …" Christy blushed with helpless embarrassment.

"I do know, darling. You can't believe you will ever be as old as I am and look the way I do." She laughed and placed her fragile arm beside Christy's. "Can you believe life can do this to a person?"

"Poor grandma."

"Poor everyone, if you think about it. Really, darling, have you ever heard of anyone getting out of life alive?" She smiled at the frightened child. "But, what of it? After this wonderful lunch there's a long afternoon to enjoy. There's cocktails, dinner and the Comedy Hour on Television. There's David's bed time massage, then my sedatives and a long sleep and then tomorrow, a lovely breakfast on the porch will get me started on another long, sweet day."

"You know, Christy, when the future is the next moment and the next, it's a very long life indeed. And I love my beautiful swimming pool. I had to fight to achieve that elegant shape. Nobody likes a bossy old woman and the contractor threatened to quit but he couldn't be happier now. He tells me he's sold scores of pools from the photos he took of this yard. Oh, it's truly beautiful!" She smiled at David Sweeney as he served her chicken salad.

"You looked like a child when you were fooling with Christy. I dare say it's the gin, but I thought of the Garden of Eden."

"Adam and Eve? Oh, man!" David avoided Christy's glowing eyes as he put food on her plate. "

"I'm a washed up bum, Helen."

"You're a very talented young man and any day now you're going to astonish the world."

"My manager hated the last two songs I sent him."

"I love your songs and so does Christy. You don't have to bother with the opinions of stupid people."

Despite the impossibility of ignoring the opinion of one's manager in the quest of fame and fortune, David Sweeney was elated by the old lady's serene confidence. She had no knowledge of music, no interest in the current music scene, most likely she couldn't remember a lyric or melody from any of his songs – but still – her optimism felt like the announcement of his imminent success. He felt gallant serving the chicken salad.

"You can laugh at an old lady all you like, but I know you're going to write a hit. But not now, if you please. Christy's visit and your splendid massages are quite enough excitement for the moment."

"I'll put off a hit if you eat some chicken salad."

"If I eat? Have you ever known me not to 'pig out' on your exquisite cooking?"

The widow smiled at Christy as she pronounced her slang, then frowned to see the girl so absent. Noisily chewing, Christy's eyes glowed as she remembered her effect on David the night before. Grafted to her body with a pounding heart, he'd been so swept away.

"Our little girl's in gaga land." Helen Reed thrust a forkful of chicken into her mouth.

"Gaga land?" David laughed. "That's like 'hell's bells' or 'corker,' 'peachy' or 'drip.' Your expressions are so sweet, Helen. Are you alright?"

David knelt by her chair as she feebly coughed. Thinking that she'd not fully swallowed the piece of chicken she'd had in her mouth, he held her hand while he looked down through the glass top of the table at Christy's long, tanned legs. Their blond hair stiffened as he gazed and when he looked up with a helpless smile, the girl was pointing, terrified at her grandmother. Helen Reed was choking.

David pulled her against him and patted her back. "Get some water, Christy." David's arm grew tired waiting for the glass and when he looked over his shoulder he saw Christy ducking into the grape arbor.

"Breathe!" he shouted into his employer's desperate face.

Her neck would go if he shook her, and her back couldn't take a pounding. Standing up, he bounced on the grass, holding her gently on his shoulder. Her lifeless weight was unexpectedly exhausting. Yelling to Christy to call an ambulance, David, relieved, felt the widow's breath on his neck.

'How strenuous," she gasped, returned limp to her chair. She touched a strand of unpinned hair and her twisted skirt.

"I'm a mess."

"You were choking."

"I put too much food in my mouth. It's her influence, her wonderful health," she gasped as her granddaughter stepped out of the arbor and sauntered up the yard, her hands full of grapes. Pausing at the fishpond, Christy gazed out across it, apparently sidetracked.

"What are you doing, you dreamy girl?"

The widow's affectionate gaze was incredulous at

Christy's distraction. With a weak clap of her hands, she ordered her granddaughter under the umbrella.

Christy tapped the old lady's lips with a grape and pushed it into her mouth. "It's the fairies' favorite food. Remember how you used to say that? I can't wait to eat tomatoes and corn from the garden. Aren't the grapes good this year?"

"That terrible taste is gone." The widow told Christy that the last few weeks she'd gotten an after taste from her meals that was horrible, as though she'd eaten rotten meat. "Now, it's gone," she smiled. "My mouth feels fresh again and I even feel better."

"Well, it is fairy food, adorable grandma, and now it's in you. Guess what?" Christy flashed a joyful smile. "It's going to be a good year for grapes. There are at least a hundred bunches ready to eat and hundreds more that are ripening. Hundreds, grandma."

"Get more grapes for supper, darling."

Holding onto David, Helen Reed buckled as she stood. After Christy had stepped back into the grape arbor she allowed David to pick her up and carry her into the house. Closing the bedroom door with a kick, he set her down on the massage table and took off her clothes.

"Look at that billiard ball!" The widow stared at the bald notch of her legs. "Look at it! Not one hair left!"

"You're ancient land. Plundered, trampled ground."

David settled her gently on her stomach and ran his thumb down her sharp spine.

"Erosion is beautiful when there's strength. Think of the planet."

Instantly eased by the touch of his hands, Helen Reed laughed and replied that the planet wasn't dying.

"Are you dying now?" He stimulated the energy routes in the old woman's spine. "Now?"

"Now, now?" She raised her head and looked back at him. "You make it sound as though you can crack into time and be some place wonderful."

"Alright! Crack into that flow."

"What flow, dear David? Where am I going?"

"To God."

"Without this tortured old body how will I keep myself together?"

"How does sunlight travel? Or lightening? You think I talk nonsense but I know you're in ignorance of your true nature." David pressed the base of her spine. "Your eternal energy."

Immensely consoled by his breezy confidence and his extraordinary hands – Helen Reed could feel in his fingers the implausible conjunction of speed and permanence – she saw Christy and David Sweeney in her garden after she was dead. In a burst of strength she rose on her arms and stared back at him.

"You've just shown me a vision of the future. Death isn't the end of life."

Thrilled with her joy, David bent and kissed her head. "Now you know."

"Oh, death is goodbye, goodbye, but LIFE! The Garden of Eden is my back yard. Your hands passed the message – oh, don't be dismayed – I've always believed in life!"

"I don't understand."

"Well, I do and it's splendid! You see," she teased him, and described the vision that had glowed in her mind. "Even eternity can be practical."

"In your mind you saw your granddaughter and me in the back yard? I don't get it, Helen. So what?"

"I also saw a baby."

The widow lied to propagate her new project, the last and greatest of her life. The birth of a child would be a certainty once Christy and David Sweeney were married and the proprietors of the Weston house.

"Cats, dogs, unicorns? What couldn't you see after three martinis and who cares?"

"I've seen how you admire Christy," the widow reproached his scorn. "You find her beautiful, intelligent – and don't you two have a grand time together."

"A grand time," David chided her. "I love your quaint, sweet words, Helen. I love your values, too – you're a moral museum – but you can't decree that Christy love me."

"So, you do love her?"

"Stop it!"

"Forgive me, David," she said, bowing her head. To his mortification, she rejoiced in his strong love. "I've decided to leave everything I own to Christy. My money, my house – everything. I want you to live here, be a sort of caretaker if you like – you'll have all the money you need and be Christy's worthy friend until the day she's old enough to marry you."

Delighting in his consternation, she smiled as she proclaimed the lovely couple an updated Adam and Eve. There would be a gallantry about their united life, and when a blonde daughter was born to them, why not call her 'Helen?'

"That's so stupid! You're sick and old, but you can't be so stupid!"

"Why am I stupid?"

"You don't have the power."

"To make Christy love you?"

As though looking straight into his heart the widow aroused his greatest fear. Striding to the window, his face burned. Christy was swimming in the pool and the trees were so powerful. In nature, energy flowed, in Christy also, but his frightened heart was becoming more like a prison, daily more alarming to the child he adored.

"Can you make me brave?" He returned to her side.

"Helen?"

"I'm not asleep," she opened her weary eyes. "It's so quiet on these hot summer afternoons. I was listening to Christy swimming in my beautiful pool. Some day, you'll hear your daughter splashing there and if her name isn't Helen, well, then, perhaps the next girl born to you and Christy will be."

"That's a no-no, Mrs. Reed." He held her hand. "The

experience of the human race dooms rule from the grave. It's insane for you to change your will!"

"You doom my plan. You! You're the problem – not philosophy! If you're offered food and a roof over your head so that for the next five years you're free to concentrate on your music why do you drag in philosophy?"

"Listen to me, Helen." David had the calm bearing of authority. I love this house. What a break for me to be able to live here for the next five years, and why shouldn't I take advantage of your momentary idiocy? After all, there's no accounting to the dead and if Christy wants to live in the house, why, I'll just pack up and go."

"You'll want to marry Christy."

"Sweet Jesus!" David rolled his eyes. "You are so out of it, so stinking loco. Your granddaughter's not an obedient dog. She's going to marry who ever she god damn well wants to marry, Mrs. Reed, and it ain't going to be me."

"She's a good loving child who will do as she's told."

"You're arrogant."

"Don't I know that you're the best man I've ever met? I want my wisdom to count for something. Why is that arrogant?"

"You and Christy are not the same person."

"Just as I do – but passionately – Christy will love you." Helen Reed smiled serenely at the dumbfounded boy.

"Why do you love me?" he whispered.

"Because you respect who you love. Don't worry," she said, acknowledging his fear, "You'll get braver."

His joy was wild. Then, in dread of disappointment, the young man exhausted Helen Reed with dismal prophecy. She couldn't command the courts; after she died she'd be thought weak minded from her illness and influenced by himself. Her daughter and son-in-law already thought he was a fortune hunter.

A weak wave indicated the contempt the widow was about to voice about Christy's parents when she heard her granddaughter start up on the drums. Bellowing in a man's voice she cursed the persistent nuisance of the young man's drums.

Every summer Helen had curbed Christy's wildness, but now she couldn't even climb the stairs. She'd known that morning that she'd never again climb up to the top of the house.

Oh, listen to that stubborn pounding! That was the compulsion in Christy passed down from her mother. Her foolish mother who'd painted like a robot all these years, just painted and painted to the neglect of everything worthwhile and, Helen Reed was sorry to say, who could not paint.

"If I can't control my granddaughter, what's the use of your divine energy? But I will!"

The weight of his hand on her back was enough to keep the widow on the massage table. He stroked her neck and promised to leave his door locked whenever he left the room.

"But you write in your room for hours at a time. She'll

be at you constantly to let her play. She won't let up. In that way Christy's just like her mother."

"Then I'll put the drums in their cases."

"Take the cases down to the cellar tonight when the child's asleep. And I don't want her diving. It's much too dangerous." Silently she doubted his competence then rested her cheek on the table. "I've just given you another duty, a terrible one, but I'll be so happy to know that Christy's summer is peaceful I'll pay extra for your trouble. I'll pay you very well."

"Christy likes to be obedient, Helen."

In his arms being carried to her bed, Helen Reed murmured that her granddaughter was a lively child who could not resist temptation.

"You must be sure to lock away those instruments!"

4

"Fuckin' mothers man, you scared me!" Surprised by David's clapping as he stood in the doorway of the attic room, the girl tumbled off the stool where she'd been drumming.

"I thought you were grandma. Can you believe the sounds she made with that chicken in her throat? I guess you thought I was running away."

Springing up from the floor, Christy sat again in front of the gleaming drums. "I heard you calling me, but I remembered how grandma's always saying that grapes are the healthiest food she eats. The awful taste in her mouth just disappeared!" Feeling more of a coward every minute since she'd deserted David in the yard, Christy blushed as he handed her a sunflower.

"For you," he bowed.

Touching the water oozing from the thick stem, the girl frowned and sucked her finger. "But, it's dead."

"It will live for days if you put it in water. It's one of the elect, Christy, picked to honor you."

"One of the what? Speaker of big words."

Christy was morose while David described predestination, finally interrupting to say that what she was hearing was shit, and that she doubted whether anyone at any time had ever really needed to feel God's stamp of approval in order to love life. What a stupid religion it was that rewarded life with death!

"What a reward for *your* beauty, huh?" Christy talked to the sunflower. "You're just living along and SLASH! You didn't even know you *were* beautiful. You didn't CARE!"

"It's just a flower." David was abashed. "There are hundreds more."

"Alive."

David stroked Christy's averted face. "I promise I'll never pick another living thing as long as I live."

"Crying?" His fingers grew wet with her tears, then his shirt as she pressed her face against his chest.

"Sweet, beautiful grandma! She gets so tired coming up the stairs and having me scream when I see her. Just now I ran away when she was choking. I couldn't stop myself – I was so scared. She must hate me too."

"You're the light of her life."

"But I betray her so much!"

"You challenge her, Christy. Your grandmother loves a good fight and she's determined to stop you."

"But, she's so weak! She toils up the stairs panting!

Her little patient smile when I shriek. Oh, why don't I just stop practicing?"

When David told Christy that he was under Helen Reed's orders to pack away his drum kit in the cellar the girl's teary despair became defiance. Her grandmother would never hear her drumming in the coal bin! There she could practice to her heart's content.

"Against my orders?" asked David.

"You can't stop me."

"I won't even try."

"You've got to try!"

Her anger surprised him. "Why?"

"You made her a promise."

His laughter enraged her and she punched his arm. "I know I promise grandma, too, but I always forget. I'm not lying," she yelled as he smiled. "When I come into your room the drums make me forget everything."

He squeezed her hand then kissed it. "I love you."

"Look at your paw – it's such an element of nature."

"Nature like in mother nature?" That he'd been around for an age, was that what Christy was thinking? That his emotions, like his skin, were worn from use?

"Emotion is always young, you know. I really do love you," he repeated.

"Only because of fucking."

"What? How can you say that when we love each other?"

"Everyone says 'fucking,' what's your problem?"

David sat down at the piano. Looking over his shoulder at Christy, he struck an indignant chord.

"You know I'm not into sex with you."

"You're not? Why not? Oh, my god – don't I turn you on?"

"Do you try to?"

"I shouldn't?" Tensing the muscles in her legs Christy studied his expression.

"No!"

"Why not?"

"Just feel what you feel."

"What do you feel?"

David played a whimsical tune and expressed his wish that he, Christy and Helen Reed could escape into some kind of time warp. The Weston house would suddenly be gone - just blip - escaping the inevitable invasion of her parents. Meanwhile they, magically displaced, could go on living exactly as they were.

"But, grandma couldn't be in pain."

"Never!"

"You'd marry me?"

"If you wanted me to."

"Trot, trot, trot in her white shoes, grandma will plan our wedding. I bet she'll redo this whole floor and just hound us to pick out paint and wallpaper and waste baskets and curtains and towels and bedspreads – I like plaid – and a rug and lamps until we go CRAZY!"

Her joyful expression became a look of terror.

"Grandma's dying!"

David yearned to know the girl's reaction to his continued tenure on Helen Reed's estate. He spoke over his playing with a beating heart. "This house will still be here, you know."

"BOMB THE HOUSE! I will!"

Lauding her loyalty even as it shamed him, David asked the girl where her grandmother would come back to, if the house she loved were a burnt out hole in the ground.

"You're talking about her spirit, right? You're older than me and much smarter," Christy stared in angry agony. "So, why do you believe in an afterlife?"

To a spontaneous tune, David sang a verse from the Bible that he'd read to Helen Reed the previous night.

"In my father's house are many mansions. If it were not so I would have told you." Christy stood touching him, the blond hairs stiff on her legs and arms.

"Is that really in the Bible – 'I would have told you?'"

Softly singing, David accompanied Christy as she sang the verse over and over again. Fright, mortification and the solemnity of pain were so clearly the error of ignorance and unhappiness, that David threw back his head and yipped.

"You sound like a dog."

"Yip-yip, yip-yip."

Christy pressed his back with hard nipples as she hugged him from behind. "If it weren't so, I would have told you. Oh, beautiful grandma. I'm so happy."

"You've always known that all this energy doesn't just disappear." David stood and gripped her knees as she leapt onto his back. "In your heart."

"My stomach, not my heart. My stomach tells me to kiss you and kiss, kiss, kiss you."

Dropping her on his bed, David sat and kept himself still as in the old days, when he watched birds in the woods. The ants and muscle cramps were as much a torment as Christy's caresses, which he must quietly absorb until the girl became a comrade in desire.

The initial intensity, the ardent mingling of moisture, air and mood made David forget the girl's way of sudden emotional departure. Then, heart thundering, he discovered Christy's pensive absence, her private eyes reflecting afternoon light off the sunny walls. He hung over her on strong, trembling arms, and she spoke:

"What's for supper?"

"Is that it? You've been thinking of food?"

Springing up, David pulled on his shorts. He tossed Christy's bathing suit onto her stomach and felt his injured pride dissolve as he watched Christy languidly raising her legs to put on her swimsuit.

"I'm starving."

"You can't be hungry."

"I can't?"

"Hey, girl – you've just finished lunch."

"Your chicken salad is so good." Christy hugged her knees to her stomach.

"Grandma ate hardly anything. There must be tons left."

"You're so greedy."

"Greedy?" Christy was dismayed. Didn't David know that sex burned off more calories than any other activity and that morning she'd been diving for hours – he'd seen her.

On his way out the door, David answered her concern with a light tap on her rump.

"Greedy," he called from the stairs.

Her butt had jiggled! Bounding up, Christy crammed her neck to see the gross new flesh that David had disgustedly prodded. Her image was too dim in the antique mirror and she rushed down the stairs to the bed where her grandmother was sleeping on her side. Her shoulder bone poked through her unpinned hair. Thick, dark, voracious hair that repelled the girl even when David was brushing it.

"Christy, darling. What's the matter?"

Ignoring her grandmother's pain as she struggled up onto her elbows and lay panting against the mound of pillows was the worst act of Christy's life.

"Look!" The girl forced Helen Reed to judge the state of her bare backside even when she saw her withering with pain. "I'm gross, aren't I? I AM!"

"Shame on you!" Sweat poured from Helen Reed's thick hair. "You look so pure and pretty."

"You don't think I'm fat?"

Hadn't Helen Reed always compared the girl to the

angels in the Italian paintings. Always? Her lips trembled as she repeated it in detail. If over the summers, Christy's great variation of size and shape hadn't disguised her essential being, then how could a few extra pounds be the cause of such worry?

"Go down and look at the Italian painting in the front hall if you want to see what you look like."

"The angel painting?"

Drawing her legs together under the sheet Helen Reed scowled as she suffered. "You're as beautiful as a renaissance angel. So was I at your age."

Christy visualized the figures she'd always thought so lovely and refined and continued to ignore her grandmother's agony as though selfishness were her ugly but temporary right.

"Those angels are thin, grandma."

"Aren't you?"

"I'm a big butt."

"Don't fret, darling. Just stop eating meat."

"What?"

"Meat's too heavy for the hot weather. It stays in the system and festers." Helen Reed groaned as she struggled onto her side. "You and I need vegetables in the summer and grapes. Oh god, this pain is hell. Get David! No, don't! It's too early. He's working on his song. Get grapes," she panted. "Run and bring me the fairies' food."

5

When he put her down in bed, Helen Reed let go her grip on the hair of her handsome masseur. "The way Barbara stared at you, David! The noise she made eating and the mess! Lord, what a mother for Christy to have!" She marked the drumbeat that rose through the house from the coal bin in the cellar where Christy was hard at her evening practice. The old woman announced her acceptance of the unhealthy pursuit if the noise "kept off her crazy daughter."

Three days ago, Barbara Stone, toting her heavy suitcase, had walked from the train station, mowed the lawn in ferocious heat and then swum until suppertime with a hideous slap and slop of water. Helen Reed, the seemingly approving mother, had spent that afternoon in the garden's shade silently phrasing her disapproval. Since then, to David, she'd cheerfully fumed.

"My daughter's in her forties and still she *will* ignore

her orange hair and her unfortunate freckles. How could she wear a shiny red tank suit? Her muscles shaking as she pounded and pounded – my poor diving board!"

David kissed her forehead as he tucked the sheet around her shoulders.

"She washed the supper dishes so fast it looked like a cartoon."

"I don't think your daughter's got a single one of your genes, Helen, but she's awfully nice."

"Oh, stop!" The widow scorned what she believed was his diplomacy. "She was god-awful – annoying you with her feeling that she's known you before. I apologize for my daughter."

He'd dreaded arrogance from Christy's mother; instead, her cordiality had warmed his heart.

"She's a good person, Helen. I like her."

"She's a terrible mother!"

Shrugging his shoulders at her mysterious anger, David gaily complimented the fiery beauty of her eyes.

"Oh, damn my dying eyes! Barbara prides herself on being a liberated woman, but with her 'I know we've met before, Mr. Sweeney,' why she's no better than the kind of gal she hates."

"It's possible we were acquainted in another life."

The yellow rage flashing from the sick woman's eyes made David feel a fly in its colossal fury. His fright embarrassed him and he shook his finger as he backed away from the bed.

"You're ugly, ma'am. Oh, shit, are you ugly!"

"How dare you?" Helen Reed sucked in her cheeks to keep from crying. "Such cruelty – out of nowhere."

Her hands fluttered against her wet eyes, then clasped together as David took a tissue and patted the springing tears. Her eyelids kept closing.

"I'm tired and irritable – oh, god, such melodramatic stuff."

"Admit you felt it."

"You turned on me, David Sweeney, and now you won't let me sleep."

"But you zapped me first – oh, come on! Admit the jealousy."

"What jealousy?" Her sleepy bewilderment was authentic and yet how could he doubt a force that the tingling in his chest was still recording?

"You're jealous of your daughter."

"Oh, no! How really wrong. Oh, David." She reached for his hand, slept for a few moments, then corrected his foolishness in an affectionate tone.

"I've known the most beautiful women of my time and never felt a trace of envy. Would you really have me jealous of my homely daughter?"

"Homely? She's cute as a bug!"

"Cute as a bug? Is that what you said, David – cute as a bug?'" Suddenly vigorous, Helen got his help to sit up and leaned back against plump pillows.

"Cute as a bug," she murmured with a grim smile.

That foolish phrase took her back years to the

summers when her daughter Barbara was a child, and her husband, young and handsome, used to play with her in the garden. Of course, then it was just an ordinary yard even with the grape arbor. The Beech tree was beautiful, but there were no flower beds or bushes, and the swimming pool was an unimaginable prospect.

"Back then, you know, my husband and I would have thought a swimming pool a Hollywood horror. We were so proud of our Yankee austerity. We thought it really sinful to try to create pleasure, but then, of course, we drank."

Tom always dashed upstairs to sweep Barbara out of her bed. She was throwing a tennis ball across the room at the age of three. The racket was almost as big as she was when Tom caught her hitting the ball at the windows and the crystal chandelier.

"Oh, I hated it, but he insisted on his time with Barbara, and I've never known a man so grieved to be cut off from his child. Even the lawyers were sorry about it – but he hadn't a leg to stand on because of his women. I've always wondered why he didn't set up a trust for Barbara instead of giving me all the money. He hated me when he went off to Texas, but he made me rich and did nothing for his adored daughter." Her gleeful malice was awful.

"She was only three years old, Helen. Your husband assumed you'd take care of her."

"What would he want me to do now?"

The compliment of her trust in his judgment was converted to self-dislike as David caught himself in stealthy study of the bedroom door. The conversation would shame him if Christy should come suddenly to see her grandmother. To her, he'd be the fortune hunter – that cynical hallucination of Lawyer Stone.

"I think you should leave me out of your family affairs," he growled.

"Aren't you going to marry Christy?" She followed his mortified gaze to the door. "Oh, listen to her drumming! How could she possibly hear us?"

"Her father despises me. To him I'm a con man trying to make a killing. Don't smile! He'll never believe that you and I are friends and that I don't want a dollar of your money. This is horrible."

"My son in law's firm is failing, he's desperate for money. But I've told you all about Jake Stone. Why are you suddenly upset about him?"

Frowning at his employer, David angrily expressed his desire to marry her granddaughter. For a moment Helen Reed's delight overcame the inertness of her diseased eyes and she tortured the masseur with the rapture of her ambition.

"Not a chance, Helen. It won't happen."

"Yes!"

"Lawyer Stone commands his daughter."

"Christy pays attention to me, you wily boy."

"She really jumps for her mother."

As Helen Reed scorned the superficiality of his observation, David sank deep beneath the un-tellable weight of his gloom. Since the first night of her mother's visit, Christy had refused to sleep with him.

"Mother's here!" she'd shrieked, struggling in his grip.

His frantic argument that Barbara Stone's drunken sleep made their attic room as safe as a highway motel resulted in the loneliest days he'd ever endured, as the girl, in brooding drum beat, mourned her mother's decline.

"Your granddaughter doesn't have her own opinions, do you know that, Helen? Until her mother came I thought Christy only worshipped you. Now, the kid's got a second god that talks out of her mouth. When her father gets here, she'll be invaded again and I'll be a sitting duck, Damn it." David pounded his fist into his palm.

"You're too stupid to talk about our sweet child as if she weren't completely normal. You obviously don't remember your own young loyalty to your parents, but once you were just like Christy."

She panted as she mentally crushed the possible truth of David's terrible accusation.

"If children don't make gods of their parents, how can they become good? I can see the famous adolescent rebellion roaring down, but this summer Christy's still a child in the garden – my garden! Last night, I so enjoyed the sounds of you two swimming as I fell asleep."

Helen Reed tugged his hair as David bent and kissed her goodnight. "Drag her out again, I say. That crazy, hell-bent girl."

Drag her out! Helen Reed's machismo and his memory

of Christy's sweaty exhaustion when he'd take the sticks from her hands aroused his flesh as he ran down the carpeted stairs and scenes of wrestled, imperious sex sped before his gleaming eyes. His sister had told him once that rape was the gift of gentlemen to women of mind. Dampened lust and the small, dim room, sound proofed by piles of ancient coal, became the site of his excruciating desire.

"Get off me!"

Lurching back as the girl shoved him, David's head hit the light bulb that hung from the ceiling at the end of a rubber cord and it swung around wildly. The careening shadows of Christy and the drums against the thick walls weakened his sexual focus; the strength of his hands dwindled when the girl threw down her sticks to wrestle him away.

"Quit!"

Flung against a mound of coal, David gaped at the delicate, steely female who'd pushed him with such force.

"What are you eating these days?"

"I eat just what grandma eats – only more."

"And meat."

"Since grandma choked on the chicken – not one bite."

"I've seen you eating meat."

"Nope."

Her recent ferocity of appetite, the huge amounts she put away made David positive that meat was the source of Christy's alarming strength.

"I have pictures in my mind of you gnawing bones. Don't be coy, girl."

His quick hands dodged her defending arms and groped to grip the jaunty solidity of her behind.

"I can feel your bones."

"I look better."

"The hell you do."

David's dismay made her feel selfish. It was as if her body were land, and what was now fenced round and private had been the village green. The grazing animals and walkers and zooming children were all pressing in doleful confusion on the strong fence painted so meanly bright.

"I feel great."

His large, warm hands pressed her head, her shoulders and slid down her arms. He touched not just the skin, but her scalp and the length of her spine, which tingled in icy ecstasy. For the past few days the increased sensitivity of her senses had delighted Christy as the reward for her recent purification – the banning of meat from her body as she consumed tons of grapes and vegetables. Her headache and nausea had been terrible the first few days of her diet, but when she read that she was feeling sick from toxins that her system was releasing with its calories of stored fat, she'd relished the pain as her cells burned off their poison.

"I can't be tired because I'm eating grandma's magic grapes."

"Come again?"

"The grapes I picked for grandma, you remember

that disgusting taste in her mouth just went away. Well, the grapes are making me strong."

Christy grinned at David and flexed the muscles of her sweetly fashioned arms. As he lectured that her duty in life was not to give into her inborn but stupid proclivity for magical belief, she placed her fingers on his larynx and relished the vibrations of his voice as they passed up her arm and into her chest.

"It's just as you say," she stopped his lips with her hand. "Really, deeply. Things are snap and flow. I eat grapes and it's electric."

"You're protein deprived." He examined the lining of her eye. "You're way, way out."

If David didn't believe that the airy structure and romantic texture of grapes were immediately imparted to her body's billions of cells, then surely, her improved appearance should speak a thousand words.

"I'm looking better these days."

"You're starving yourself out of the most beautiful figure I ever saw."

"Oh, stop!" Christy ducked her head to hide her pleasure.

"You're dangerously beautiful."

"More beautiful than mother?"

"Are you crazy?"

"I'm bad," the girl murmured as she blushed. "I could never be more beautiful than her because she's so beautiful, so smartly beautiful like a writer or doctor or business woman. I like the looks of intelligent women. I can see why men yearn to make love to them and then read a book they wrote or look at one of their paintings. I'd be sleeping with her too," she reassured the mystified young man.

"Sleeping with who?"

"My mother."

David's eyebrows strained towards the top of his head as if to create more cranial room for understanding.

"I don't blame you for sleeping with my mother." Christy shouted as though he'd gone deaf from bewilderment. "She's so beautiful."

"She's not beautiful!"

David smiled at her relief, then countered her reproach with the idea that Barbara Stone was beautiful, but not as beautiful as Christy. No sooner was he relieved by the triumph in her eyes, than her misery bade him seek words of comfort.

"Your mother's nice looking – really nice eyes behind those wacky glasses – oh, Christy, honey, what's the problem?"

"My mother *is* beautiful."

"She's very appealing." David bowed to the girl's bewildering hostility with a shrug. "She looks like an eccentric child."

"All the children are in love with David Sweeney."

"Fuck you!" he gasped at the whip of her hatred.

"And fuck you, ass bone, because my mother's got a crush on you."

"You're crazy."

Christy pointed at the barred window opposite the drum set and wept. "I look out through those bars and all day long I see your feet and then her feet going back and forth – your legs then her legs because she's following you like a dog and you don't even think she's beautiful."

"You're stupid because you're starving! Don't you see the painting gear? I'm the servant in this house and your mother's captive model. She told me that she'd gone stale this winter working off photographs. We hardly say a word to each other and once in a while she helps me out with my work." Christy's accusatory sorrow made him frantic.

"For god's sake! I don't ever think about your mother."

"You're mean."

"She's a painter, Christy. She doesn't impose herself – she paints. Oh, come here!" David clutched the girl as though she were physically departing and bent her head back with the force of his kiss. Her dismay as she caught her breath and her pushing arms made him desperate, and he used all his strength to kiss her again.

"Mother!"

"What?"

She held him off. "Mother's here!"

Following her panicked gaze, David saw Barbara Stone standing in the doorway. She carried a whiskey and wore a white cotton tee shirt that covered her body to the top of her legs. As she smiled and brought the glass to her lips, the shirt dragged up and exposed her genitals.

69

"Mother and Christy are swans." The painter tipped David a friendly nod and added that she was not a swan, which was alright with her, except that she wished some man would adore her as David adored her daughter.

"He *does* adore you, darling." She turned her sweet, mournful gaze on Christy's burning face. "And why are you embarrassed? I was watching you in the yard and I never saw a girl more in love in my life, Christy."

"Let me congratulate you." She exhorted, staggering badly as she stepped towards her daughter.

"Oh, you silly child. Oh, dear! You look so prissy."

"I am prissy."

"Lying toad! I brought you up to crash about with boys. My god, did mother fume about the football. I'm hungry, but let's swim before dinner."

Barbara took her daughter's hand forcefully and pulled her out to the poolside, as David followed the pair with marked trepidation, even suspicion.

Barbara slid languidly into the pool and began to swim.

"Jump in!"

"I'm putting on my suit," responded her daughter.

Her vigorous kicking kept Barbara Stone from hearing David Sweeney's frightened counsel to Christy. Seized with a sudden instinct, he begged her not to subject herself to the danger of her mother's intoxication. After Christy had dived in, he lay down on the diving board, stretching his arms out over the black water.

"Over here!" he cried out. "Christy – swim!"

"Your lover is calling you!" said Barbara Stone in a gay, malicious voice.

"He's not my lover."

"I'll bite you, little girl."

Christy's voice shook with fear as she told her mother that she'd return the favor.

"Duck under, Christy! Swim under here – TO ME!"

"Want your boyfriend? Oh, be my guest."

Barbara Stone dove after her daughter, the waves of their commotion rapidly resounding on the sides of the pool, wetting David Sweeney's hanging hands. Then he saw Christy emerge at the steps, a long ribbon of scarlet running down her leg. There was a quick shriek and feet slapping on the flagstone. Yelling after her on the diving board, peering towards the house, David suddenly felt strong, cold hands round his ankles.

"Pull me out, please," Barbara gasped.

"You hurt Christy."

"Do it!"

Diving, swimming, running – an explosion of flight landed David at the top of the house outside the bathroom door, shaking at the vision of what had surely been blood as Christy ran from the pool. Calling to her, his skin shivered from the mother's avid clasp.

The girl let him in, locked the door behind them, then stepped up on the toilet seat and twisted her body to see her backside in the mirror that hung from the opposite wall. Peering over her shoulder, her bathing suit fell onto her feet, and she groaned at the image of her punctured rump, poking the meager flesh with cruel fingers.

"Fucking mothers, it's fat!"

"Stop that! You'll infect it."

"Quit!" She pushed away his hand. "This is punch massage! Punch, punch, punch it off – ugly fat!"

"Are you crazy? Do you want a putrid wound?"

The blood seemed to surprise the girl and she looked curiously at the teeth marks bleeding beneath David's protective hand."

"How'd I get that?"

"How'd you get your ass bitten off?"

"That's a bite?"

"You felt it, Christy. Stop pretending."

"I thought she'd only pinched me."

"Didn't you feel it?" David took a bottle of hydrogen peroxide from the medicine chest and soaking a wad of cotton gently cleaned the punctured skin.

"You must have, poor darling."

"Now, I do." The liquid foamed in the wounds. "It aches."

"Your mother's crazy, Christy. She should be put down."

"Drinking makes her a dog, you mean."

"A mad dog."

"Then I need a rabies shot."

"You're staying with me tonight."

"No way!"

"You need protection."

"From you, man."

"ME?" As he struggled to respond, Christy stepped up on the closed seat of the toilet and studied once again the reflection of her buttocks with fastidious disdain.

"Meat makes meat."

"What does that mean?"

"Meat's too heavy for the hot weather. It stays in the system and festers."

"Festers? What's up with you, Christy? You keep saying stupid things."

"Everyone knows that meat is bad for you. It makes you fat."

Revolted by her dainty self-satisfaction, David sarcastically asked the girl if she knew of any substance, that wouldn't, when eaten in abundance, pile on the flesh?

"Grapes don't make meat."

"They're loaded with calories."

"But they don't make fat."

Christy's eyes, with a weird glow, spoke of the magical power of her grandmother's grapes. The annulment of awful tastes had been the introduction to even greater wonders. Could David believe that she'd discovered a variation of the law that equates substance with energy? As the days went on, her energy had grown by eating less.

In the late afternoon her drumming didn't make

her tired and even cloudy days glowed with energy. What David had told her – that the actual structure of reality is electrical – she could now see, and feel too, exquisitely.

"The human eye can't see electrons, Christy, absolutely not!"

"You look scared. What's the matter?"

"You're hallucinating because you're starving. You need food, darling."

"I do?" Infected by his fear, Christy slipped her arms through the straps of her bathing suit and followed David down the stairs to the kitchen.

"I'm not hungry for meat." Perched on a stool beside the stove she watched the muscles of his back and his swinging hair as he fried a steak.

"I'll go pick some grapes."

"Keep yourself indoors, girl." He put the steak on the table and drew out two chairs. Her leg swung against his as he sat. "The crocodile's still in the pool. Soy sauce?"

"It's gross! You hardly cooked it."

"You like your meat rare."

"I want grapes."

"Eat this."

Loathing his sweat smell and the blood smell of the meat as his fingers poked steak between her teeth, her mouth was suddenly full of saliva and wetness flooded her underpants. Swallowing, she sucked in her cheeks in a passion of hunger.

"More," she moaned.

David cut his finger as he sliced up the steak and

when she'd eaten the last bit of meat and the crisps of fat she popped his bloody finger into her mouth and watched him with filmy eyes as she sucked and sucked.

"Wild, beautiful girl, I love you. You're a rich girl, too. You know that? Oh, yes," he crooned, "you're to inherit your grandmother's money and live in this house with me. It's her plan, Christy – her practical immortality."

"Speak English, please." She dried his finger with the napkin.

"A house exchange is going on. Weston for our minds. She wants all her possessions to remind us of her, day in and day out."

"It's like that bible thing we were playing – about God's mansions."

Christy's wary attention grew joyous. "I'll be wearing sweaters in Weston! I'll go to that big, brick high school and do my homework in the kitchen while you cook. We'll talk about grandma and we'll keep all her clothes with their wonderful smell. We won't change the furniture around or recover anything so that we can repeat forever her fuss about the leather chairs and the shabby French couch. It will be cozy – like she's just upstairs, taking her nap."

Rushing kisses on David's smiling mouth, Christy was suddenly white in the face.

"My father," she beseeched him.

"Here?" His frightened eyes raced round the kitchen.

"His firm is failing. He's waiting for grandma's money."

"Are you crazy?"

"Don't look like that – it's not what you think."

"It's worse," the masseur declared when told that the lawyer was eager to rescue the inherited millions from their present frivolous use. "Your father thinks he's more important to the world than Helen Reed. He's a fool!"

"Grandma loves her swimming pool, but my parents say she's wrong to spend so much money when she's dying."

David's disdain exposed her own and Christy trembled with dismay.

"They'd be glad if grandma were dead right now."

"God damn it!"

"It's not their fault. It's what they believe in."

"Give me a break."

"They kill themselves working, working, working because they want to be happy. But, listen, just breathing can make grandma's day. Adorable grandma!"

The bomb of death, its black explosion, had not yet occurred to her mother. She was so into habit that only the unanswered ringing, ringing, ringing when she made her regular Monday morning call to Weston would make her realize the catastrophe and then – she would be so sad.

David kissed her mournful face. "You'd be living here in Weston with me and *you* can comfort your mother. Isn't that a good thing to think about?"

"I'm just a child." Terrified, she pushed him away. "How can I comfort my mother and give my father money. Grandma can't do this!"

"Surely, she can protect you with her money, Christy. She always has."

"Oh, she has!"

"She's wanted to. You're the light of her life."

Her guilt was awful. "Beautiful protection! This house with all her things and smells and YOU!" She hurt his fingers with her frantic strength. "My father won't take money from me!"

He turned away from her untenable conflict. "Then go tell your grandmother how you feel."

"But I do want to live here with you."

"Make up your mind," he growled then cursed her kin for the warfare they waged on Christy's soil.

"I am occupied territory," Christy admired his insight. "The parents are here and grandma. Fuckin' mothers, man, I got no mind to make up."

"Tell Helen!"

"Grandma's asleep."

Lifting Christy, he carried her to the head of the stairs.

"Go on!" he nudged her with a stony jaw. "Tell your grandmother you don't want her money. *Go on!*"

6

At the break-up of the grim evening meeting, Hal Busby, the firm's head, took Jake Stone by the arm and walked him into his office. He coughed as he lit a cigarette and swore into the explosion of smoke.

"What the blue Jesus is going on with Helen Reed? Charlie Vance tells me she's selling stocks to pay some scoundrel off the street a fortune to cure her. She's being healed through massage, she tells Charlie – restored to life."

The old man's weak legs dumped his weight onto the leather chair. Coughing bursts of smoke, he frowned up at Jake. "What do you and your wife know about this?"

"Helen tells Barbara that the young man's touch could jump start the dead."

Their eyes met with a gleam of merriment then the old man glared. Having founded the law firm with Helen Reed's husband, Hal Busby had survived his partner by a decade. Ferociously brilliant, he was a goad of terror to the score of younger partners.

"Pigmies," he taunted them. They were all freeloaders who could neither pull in the business as he had done, nor do the tough work to keep it.

Jake knew the economy was bad and business stagnant, and that brains and the ability to bring in work had not declined one whit with his generation of partners. Yet these undoubted facts could not protect him from the shame and self doubt that assaulted him in Hal Busby's irritable presence. Back in the meeting, when he spoke out for a merger with one of the law firms that were feasting like sharks in the bloody world of corporate takeovers, he'd felt like a terrified boy. Now, answering to the old man about his mother-in-law, Jake Stone was dismayed to feel the heat of his face.

The wealth of the dying woman was another site for sharks, he told Busby, alluding to his counsel at the partners' meeting. Helen Reed had dismissed as pedantry her doctor's diagnosis that her cancer had gone into spontaneous remission. How were her caring circle to keep combating her joy in living?

"He's a masseur? He touches Helen Reed all over? God help us!" the old man growled. "But the woman's been magnificent – such a lady – and beautiful."

"Helen is still beautiful."

"But pudding," Hal Busby tapped his temple. "A sitting duck, a patsy for some god damned punk who's after her money. Damn it, Jake, if you can't control the situation then get your wife into action."

"Barbara's in the country now, sir, but as you know, for years now, she and her mother have been estranged."

"Don't 'no' me to death, Jake." Coughing again, the old man waved his partner from his presence. "You're going to need Tom Reed's money to live on for a period. I warn you."

To compensate for the current decline of business, the cut in the partners' draw was to be so drastic that only the senior partners, men free of family expenses, or the wealthy few of Jake's contemporaries, could possibly afford to subsidize a failing firm. And it was absolutely the wrong approach, Jake Stone felt – a weak and frightened approach.

In his passion to revive the old partner's common sense, Jake stepped back into his office, loudly telling him that if the firm was un-competitive they must adapt to the changing economy as the new firms were doing. Their golden reputation was a powerful lure that must be cast to the slew of opportunists now practicing law.

"We've got to do as the Romans do, sir, or we're not going to make it."

In passionate irritation, the old partner crushed out his cigarette and fiercely pinched Jake's strong arm. *Kidder and Black* had gone that route and in a year, their respected competitor had disappeared.

"That was a boarding, not a merger and as the senior partner of this firm, I will not allow you younger men that decision. You're dangerously wrong here, Jake. You're way out of line."

The senior partner tottered as Jake pulled from his clasp. He steadied him and was again in argument when Hal Busby, pale with fury, bade him 'good night.'

Forty years old and for seven years the old man's partner, Jake Stone was dismissed from his presence like a child. On his way from his office to the street, he was unaware of the greetings of his colleagues and their startled looks. When he'd walked two blocks and looked back at the towering building, it upset him not to remember riding down on the elevator or walking through the lobby, as though the insult of Hal Busby's dismissal had blown out his memory.

The rage boiling inside him against the old man's imperial command was shocking. For fourteen years, the supreme power of the older men had made him neither resentful nor impatient. The financial importance of the cases, their fearful complexity, made responsibility more dreadful than glorious and only a fool couldn't see that imagination, even a genius for law, was an airy advantage compared to experience. To Jake, experience hard won plainly justified the arduous ascent to authority.

A robust, ambitious, cheerful man who worked hard to deserve his drink, and who loved, when drinking, to ponder his work, Jake Stone was happy to be humble. His mind patiently mastered the totality of a subject, and his colleagues, repelled by such laborious exertion, proclaimed him to be deep. It was evident from his fine success that he was deep enough for the world of business, yet in the world of expressed emotion – his wife was a painter – he daily felt himself at sea.

Jake was generous by temperament and by principal ideal, loyal. He considered the law firm not just to be the field of his ambition but the extension, through his partners, of every trait of intellect and character he possessed. As in his days of college crew, he loved the amplification of merged effort and will. His current opinion of the firm's wrong course – because he wasn't selfish or slavish – made him vociferous. On a ship, in a fog, a huge bulk looming, the situation couldn't be more urgent.

"Look at this," he murmured suddenly, his train of thought interrupted.

Jake stepped off the curb to stare in a window without blocking the crowd. In large red letters, a sign announced "Abogado." Staring into the cheerfully jammed office, he discovered an orange cat asleep on a file cabinet as an Hispanic man, briskly typing at a desk, turned his head and smiled. He got up and opened the door.

"Got a problem?" he asked with nervous kindness.

"I'm admiring your office. I suppose you're pretty busy."

"Everybody's got a problem. Lots of problems. Eviction, working papers, jail, death." His brows lifted above alert, patient eyes, the Abogado waited to hear the nature of Jake's dilemma.

"Are you the whole show?" Jake admired the eccentric office. "I have so many partners."

The man's tired face flashed with pride. "I like to do things right."

"And you keep afloat?"

With a quick laugh the lawyer rolled his eyes at imagined disaster. "I've got a family – two kids. My wife works and we make it."

Walking away, Jake pointed at the tower of his office building. "I work up there."

Cheerfully envious, the Abogado shouted after Jake that he was doing alright.

"Hard times," Jake called back. "Wish me luck."

"You crazy man! You're the king."

Up to an hour ago, Jake Stone would have accepted the respect of the "Abogado" as perfectly reasonable. Like a warship, the massive tower where Jake worked towered over the two-bit businesses that lined both sides of the commercial street. Holding open the door of the subway station, as Jake looked back, the precarious existence of the numberless concerns now took on the aspect of adaptability. He imagined watching the Abogado's buoyant survival above the sinking prow of Reed and Busby – the insulated will of the old partner a lethal anchor in the grinding sea.

On the subway to his uptown apartment, Jake heard the shriek of speed as the sound of his humiliation. The knuckles of his broad hands were white on the edge of the plastic seat while the frequent flash of his angry smile unnerved the passengers who sat opposite him.

In the entire judicial system, as far as Jake knew, that attractive Hispanic lawyer who'd called him a king could not be leveled as he had just been by his partner. Not even a judge on the Supreme Court of the United States would dare so strip another lawyer of his pride. How dare Hal Busby? How dare he preempt the leadership of the firm on the basis of his distrust of the younger partners? What grounds had he for his distrust?

In litigation alone Charlie Nash, Bruce Roseman and Jim McClean regularly won cases for the firm. He, himself, had recently wrested an enormous settlement for a major client and had the old man said one word about it? And, come to think of it, Hal Busby never encouraged or congratulated his partners, as if in silent declaration that it wasn't they who were winning the victories, but the splendid reputation of the firm.

Running up the subway steps to an elegant street a few blocks from his apartment house, rage burned in Jake's chest. The entire conversation about Helen Reed was a torture to remember. How dare Hal Busby inform him that he now needed a dead man's fortune to survive as if being wealthy was the bedrock issue here, and not the degrading and unnecessary subsidy of a vital firm? Damn it!

The handsome red brick building where Jake had been so proud to buy a large apartment looked vulnerable in its ornate bulk – plainly top heavy for a bad blow. A grand apartment, it was bedlam to Helen Reed, who had for years refused to visit what she scornfully described as her daughter's dusty art gallery. But it was so expressive of his wife's blithe spirit and the spontaneity of Christy, his daughter, that it delighted Jake to afford its costly rent.

Before his affluent partnership in the triumphant Wall Street firm, scholarships and part-time jobs had sustained him during the long years of his education and grafted frugality to his natural generosity. Despising this trait, he realized that only serious money could release him from an exhausting materialism. Then he met her, Barbara Reed. She was a painter.

Two decades previously at a gallery, a huge canvas with fierce shapes and color had attracted him, along with the intensity of a red haired young woman who stood with her chin pushed forward and her finger pointing as though in argument with the work. Turning her head, she looked at him through cock-eyed glasses and used one corner of her mouth to quickly smile.

She could cut up a thing so slick and sentimental with a knife, she said, or should have done so in the privacy of her own studio. His amazement that she should see ugliness in a painting that inspired him, quickly turned her chagrin to excitement that he was proud of his effect on her.

That a sophisticated painter would take heart from the response of his emotions excited him more than her surprising connection to the law firm where he'd recently been hired as a clerk.

She was the daughter of Tom Reed, the firm's founding partner. Excitedly, he pitted himself against her dread that marriage and motherhood would intimidate her struggles to paint. His wealth, unlike her father's, would not provoke her horror of possession and deadening social ritual. Her dedication to painting could burn up his money like fuel. In fact, he repeatedly declared, thrilled by the romantic contract between them, she would justify his overpaid work in the way of a cause.

There had never been an evening when Jake's first steps through his apartment's front door hadn't presented a gratifying contrast to his office tower – the pride of his own lobby announced in marble and mirror. Christy's bike to get by or a newly painted canvas, the dented walls and ripped lampshades and all about a furry dust as though the furniture were pets.

Tonight, Jake's foot kicked an envelope that had been thrust under the door. His heart jumping up his throat, he read the landlord's notice, then stormed down the hall to his wife's empty studio.

"We're evicted, Barbara." A mass of painted canvases absorbed his frightened voice. "Hal Busby's got my money and we're damn well screwed."

Jake's tone was conversational despite the two weeks that he'd been living alone. "I've got to ask your mother for a loan."

He stood before his wife's unfinished painting of Helen Reed, his fright disdained by her cruel eyes.

The portrait of the matriarch sitting with her granddaughter in the Weston garden was intended by his wife to honor their similar beauty. The survival of this beauty as Christy lived was to reconcile the old woman to her step through death's door. But a month passed as Barbara painted a face that could only make Helen Reed add vindictiveness to the list of injurious qualities that she knew her daughter by.

She was a good painter, Jake had been shouting into his wife's nightly gloom. Unlike shallow crowd pleasers, she had depth.

Ah, her work was junk boiling up from a depth that didn't matter was his wife's weary answer. She'd forgiven Helen Reed's intolerance and her cruel partiality for Christy. What was the point of her victory over the damn jealousy and rage if her mother's love wasn't to be won or even her praise?

Once, chiding his wife's sentimentality, he had made her weep. The great success of her rebellion, her painting, had set Helen Reed to gnashing her teeth.

As his eyes glanced between the two beautiful faces presenting good and evil in angry declaration, in his mind he could hear Helen Reed bellow:

"Damn you, Jake!"

During her surprise visits to their apartment she'd railed against the buy and break philosophy she discovered. Buy and break, dust and holes, how could Jake compete in a prestigious firm if he couldn't ask his clients to dinner in a gracious house? Could he even entertain at a restaurant with a wife all paint-spotted like a nursery schooler?

When Jake declared that he'd married an artist and had no right to make such claims, Helen dismissed him as a fool. He must have been born yesterday to indulge his wife's dreadful affectation as talent, and he would pay for it when his harum-scarum apartment and his brilliant career crashed about his ears.

"Your world is gone, Helen. You and Hal Busby don't know the score anymore. If I had millions and Barbara entertained every night, I'd be no less endangered by stupidity than I am now. Believe me, I see what to do."

As the phone in Weston rang and rang, Jake glanced at the wall clock. Eight to eight thirty was the expected time of his evening call and he endured his embarrassment as each barrage of noise invaded the peace of the distant, dignified country house. Finally, Helen answered, delivering some unlikely news.

"What? What did you say, Helen?"

The mannish, cultivated voice of his mother-in-law repeated that his wife, although she didn't herself know it, was head over heels in love with the young and handsome David Sweeney.

"When hell freezes over, Mrs. Reed, that elegant daughter of yours will fall for a masseur."

The steely silence of her response surprised Jake Stone in his accustomed habit of snobbish flattery. Inspired to disguise his admiration of his wife's social eminence, his mother-in-law had always received his wise cracks as compliments. Now, to his placating laugh came a gruff command. On Christy's birthday, she wanted her daughter under his control.

"The first train in the morning, the milk train, will get you to Weston before Barbara is out of bed and causing havoc in my household."

"Havoc, Helen? What do you mean?"

"No sooner awake than she is traipsing after David Sweeney – your wife is appalling!"

At seven o'clock as the lad drove to the village to buy the morning paper, she was beside him in the car, continued his mother-in-law. Returning downstairs having brought up her breakfast tray, he would find Barbara waiting to drink her coffee with him. He could expect to chlorinate the water in the pool, clip the hedges and prepare the noonday meal embarrassed and obstructed by Barbara Stone's mooning presence. The only time in the last ten days that the young man hadn't been dogged by her lovesick daughter, was during the hours after lunch when he gave Helen Reed her massage behind the closed door of her bedroom.

"Oh, Helen, really." Jake chuckled while patting down the short bristling hairs on the back of his head. "She's taking over plans for Christy's birthday and giving him a friendly hand with his chores. Or, she's made him the model of a new painting."

"That's it!" A strong laugh released his tension. "She's taking advantage of a captive model. Come on," he argued against the phone's angry silence. "You know Barbara can't stop herself from painting. She's the genuine artist type."

"The yard and house are littered like a slum with somber sketches of David, David, David. You are a fool, Jake, to consider such compulsion the mark of an artist."

"Ye God, you're so predictable." Jake's fear of David Sweeney, and dread that Barbara could be disloyal, disappeared as he recognized the old woman's jealousy of her daughter's striving spirit. As Helen Reed described the coal bin as Christy's refuge from the sight of her mother's pathetic schoolgirl 'crush,' Jake pictured the young man's borrowed drum set in the gloom.

Indeed, the familiar figures disclosed by the old lady's rancor roused Jake's paternalistic pride and he announced, as he stood to hang up the phone, that bright and early the next morning he would get his two 'gals' under control.

"But, Helen, Barbara knows I call her at eight o'clock. Has she gone to bed?"

"Your wife drank too many whiskeys at dinner!" That evening in a sexual stupor, Helen continued, she had cornered David Sweeney, forcing the oppressed young man to fly up the stairs to the safety of his bedroom.

"Wait! Helen, wait, please! I absolutely reject this account of Barbara's behavior. It is just not true."

"Are you calling me a liar?"

"Absolutely not!" Panicked by this picture of his wife, Jake could not stop himself from shouting this rousing word. "Absolutely not! But Helen, he described Barbara to you, right? HE told you, he? You didn't see Barbara crawling around with your own eyes."

Helen Reed informed Jake that while she'd taken a turn for the worse – the terrible pain in her back was now keeping her in bed – as yet there was nothing wrong with her ears. They had blazed from David Sweeney's scandalous account.

"He's lying to you! In the most cynical fashion. Why would he lie to you? WHY? To make himself rich, I'm sorry to say."

Helen Reed admitted that she paid a fortune for the relief of miraculous massage but by the standards of her class, David Sweeney, when she died, could only consider himself a little ahead of the game. Oh, no! No, no, no! The youth valued his job. He enjoyed their endless talks and he enjoyed – her endurance was the proof – the hours of work on her body.

"My god, that's awful!"

Helen Reed laughed to disguise her anger at her son-in-law. "What's so disturbing about that?"

"You're not some sales girl to be touched all over! I'm going to set him straight, Helen. He's way out of line."

"Oh, god – another patriarch," bantered Helen Reed, as rage turned her heart to ice. His outburst took her back thirty years to the time when her husband, another righteous fellow, had forbidden her to swim in public because he thought the exposure of her aging body had become undignified. Downright forbidden to swim at the club or the beach, and she'd towed the line.

"I am a righteous fellow, Helen. I apologize." Excited

by her intimate, teasing tone, Jake stood smiling in his wife's studio.

"Oh, you mustn't apologize!" But it troubled the widow not a little that, sight unseen, Jake would dare to challenge the many facts that formed her impression of the lad. What wise insight was his that contradicted her vital belief in the boy's goodness? Holding back her dreadful pain, his hands must like what they touch.

"Ill health repels the young. You'd know that, Helen, if you weren't so sick." Never hesitant to voice an opinion, the widow's longed for respect intoxicated Jake and made him fatally frank. "Your David Sweeney is indicted by the timeless truth, my dear – not by me."

The stifled rage of her once dependent life now seethed beneath the widow's affectionate teasing. "If you're talking foolishness like the 'timeless truth.' Then you'd better take advantage of the long holiday weekend and get as much rest as you can."

"I'll rest when I've booted your young scoundrel out the front door."

"You'll be killing me then," she said, "because I can't live without the daily infusion of love from his hands."

"Never mind!" The lawyer boomed, intensely embarrassed. "You've been shamefully influenced and you've needed my advice. It's not my fault – I've been so damn busy – but I'll make it up to you. If I catch the milk train, I'll be at your service by breakfast time tomorrow."

"Excellent!" the Widow responded, as her hidden hatred leapt and raced. "For breakfast we'll have Polish smoked ham, tomatoes from the garden, country eggs and fresh ground coffee – but only after you've taken a swim in my beautiful swimming pool."

"If the pleasure from its cold, sparkling water doesn't annul your worries about the diminished market value of my property, then I'll consider your irritating prudence concerning my new project."

"You're a rigorous Yankee, my darling, not some showy arriviste," quipped Jake. "Naturally, I'll enjoy a plunge on a scorching day, but I'm determined to make you see how you've struck out with this damn silly puddle."

"Well, well, well, I didn't know it had happened ..."

"What's happened, Helen?"

For the second time that night his honest, blunt force had reminded her of Tom Reed and the deference once paid to him by herself and the score of his associates.

"My son-in-law has become number one in the law firm – that's what has happened."

"Hal Busby doesn't listen to me, and you put in that swimming pool. And now you apparently want to put in a tennis court?" Tomorrow he would see the influence of his new power as she judged his advice with an open mind.

"I'm looking forward to hearing your thoughts on that. It's my last 'little' project!"

She was secretly pleased, as she hung up the phone in

her country house, that her hypocritical compliments had inflated to folly her son-in-law's pride.

In a flood of mental scenes as Jake drank and packed his suitcase for the long summer weekend, he saw himself being courageous with Hal Busby. Imperious, irritable, the old partner had listened to him, then mortified his colleagues with his lashing praise. Jake Stone wasn't a pigmy like them! Endowed with the energetic brilliance of the old giants, Jake was the bedrock of *Busby and Reed*.

"Oh, Helen," Jake murmured as he poured another drink. "Oh, my darling, Victorian gal."

7

She was dolefully tired and the sun hurt her eyes, but by seven o'clock in the morning, Helen Reed required the masseur to do her hair, dress her and carry her down to the terrace. She denied her pain to the worried young man and began berating her daughter, who was sitting under the yellow umbrella, for her nightly drunkenness. The bite mark she'd discovered last night as Christy stood in frightened silence – how dare she? Her behavior was so wrong and ugly.

Christy drumming, Barbara swimming, a speeding train bringing Jake from the city: the widow panted in the umbrella's yellow shade and ordered David to bring breakfast to her daughter, as he set down her scrambled eggs and coffee.

"You look ghastly, Barbara. I hope you won't be sick on Christy's birthday." She frowned at her daughter who stood in the brutal sun moving her hands in and out of the umbrella's yellow shade.

"Stop fiddling, won't you?"

"The yellow light on your skin scared me."

Barbara Stone admired the thoughtfulness of the young man, who'd considered the obstruction of the umbrella's pole and the hostility of the company when he'd placed a second placemat at the greatest distance from Helen Reed. She sat down with a sad smile.

"I thought you were a goner."

"I am." The widow watched her daughter weep with calm eyes. She found them an amusing pair. Here was the dying mother, happy as a clam, and it was the daughter, with a good half of her life yet to enjoy, who was crying her eyes out.

"I love you." Embarrassed by her mother's dour imperturbability, Barbara Stone smiled and swallowed eggs. "I love the way you dress – ever so spruce."

"You don't care about clothes."

"Not for myself or Christy, but I love your style."

"Liar."

"I love your spiffy look."

"You? Even when you were little you insulted me with your damn dingy clothes. It was always a struggle to get you into a dress – an exhausting struggle. You laugh, as you always have, but I'll never forgive you for taxing my strength. No!"

She glared as her daughter called her a hypocrite.

"How dare you say that to me?"

"You're tired this morning, mother. So am I."

Barbara Stone's calm and kindly tone infuriated the widow. Her homely daughter whose crush on a handsome youth was exposing a pathetic immaturity could only feign such composure.

"You're not tired – oh, you're the hypocrite – you're hung over!"

"A little," she shrugged with an easy smile. I'm on vacation, you know."

David Sweeney came out of the house and fetched the skimmer from the pool house. Her daughter's shining concentration as she watched him scooping leaves from the pool, her ever-ready sketch pad taken up from the grass, inflamed the widow and she attacked the shameless passion.

"No, no, no, mother. Really, no. I find I can draw your masseur and he lets me. That's all you're seeing. Although I can't blame you for the look of the thing" Barbara Stone raised friendly eyes from the pad. "If you knew the hell I was in this winter – my bad work filling up the joint – you'd understand what it means to feel simple and quick."

Her daughter's generous response as she intensely sketched intimidated the widow and her own sudden deference – she was bowing her head – brought back her memory of being a wife. Again she was furious at her daughter's unaccountable confidence.

"You dress and act like a man, but you're not successful the way men are. Oh, no!"

"Thank you!" The eager concentration of the painter yielded one gay glance.

"You'd be selling your work if you were as good as you think you are."

"Look, mother." Barbara Stone held up the pad to hide her blushing face.

"You've made him look like an angel." The widow rejected the amplification of her own opinion. "He's neither so pure nor so generous."

"I'm so aware of him – just living."

"You're in love and ridiculous. I'm ashamed for you."

"Three generations of Yankee women are plain done in by my mother's masseur." Barbara Stone pressed her heart with its pain of longing.

"Always vulgar."

"No! If my fascination were sexual you wouldn't see me following him around with a pad and pencil. I'd be hiding, like Christy, in the coal bin. No, wait! Please!" Smiling, the daughter described the dream feelings that were invariably induced by the young man's presence.

"I feel as though he were physically huge, although I can certainly see that he's just the size he is. The other morning, by the fish pool, in this conscious hallucination of his grandeur, I got to suddenly feeling child-like and radiant. I felt my goodness with wonder as though I'd been endorsed by a god."

"You're drinking, Barbara. Don't deny that you're drunk every night."

"What?"

"Your entire generation has sex on the brain. It's

everywhere – the television, the movies, the popular music blaring away. But it's not in this house, I promise you. *Not* in David Sweeney, not in my granddaughter! It's in you!"

"What's happening?"

"It's your own lust you're seeing – not my darling children."

For a moment, Barbara Stone thought the devil was looking out of her mother's eyes. A lifetime of ignored desire was purulent pain in a yellow blaze.

"Your granddaughter's a beautiful young girl and she's in love with David Sweeney."

"Ah, Barbara, you bit a kid with a crush."

When she heard that she'd sunk her teeth into Christy's rump while they'd been taking a night swim, Barbara Stone began a sketch of the pool. Laughing, she told her mother that she was hoping to draw a memory because not one detail of what she was hearing was in her mind.

"You're drinking too much."

"Not over my quota."

"Traipsing after David, jealous of Christy, I imagine you're not sexually happy with your husband. I'm sorry," she interrupted her daughter's embarrassed silence. I remember so well your adolescent declaration that you would never endure an unromantic marriage."

"Well, I wouldn't and I don't."

"Men's ambition, their worry – in less than three years, your father's passion became a longing for sleep. It's life, darling."

Helen Reed's gentle tone and endearment weakened her daughter's defiance and she asked her mother, longing for her love, if life wasn't what one made it.

"Life laughs in your face, I'm sorry to say. You try to change everything while I'm just a little person and look who's jealous of their daughter? Not me, my darling."

Ambushed, Barbara Stone hooted her pain at the sky. Helen Reed's tenderness had momentarily roused the unconscious apparition that ruled the painter's heart – her mighty mother – a golden god.

"I'm not jealous of Christy."

"You've become two people, my dear. Every night my household meets a horror. Oh, yes, you're the six o'clock horror show. Now, let me see how you've managed to make my beautiful swimming pool look ugly." She held out her hands for the pad.

"Why, it's just what it is, isn't it? How straightforward, Barbara. There's none of your conceited meaning here. This is the way you should always draw – you'd make millions. Say, could you do a sketch of a tennis court if I describe where I want it built?"

Barbara Stone's flying hands obeyed her mother's demanding clarity.

"Oh, say! It tucks right into the hill. I've been stewing over just where a tennis court should be built to the best advantage of play and appearance, and now, thanks to you, clever girl, I can call up Mr. Salvadore this morning. I wouldn't wonder if he couldn't start today, your drawing's so precise. I really thank you, Barbara. I'm so up for a little improvement."

"I should sign it 'the six o'clock horror.'"

Her daughter's melancholy resentment amused the old woman. "You're still blaming the messenger – at your age."

"After all these years of trying and trying, to think that this silly little sketch should win your praise – I want to die."

"That's my department."

"No! Come on!" Barbara Stone ignored her mother's joke. "You've branded my dedication as immoral and it isn't fair! I'm not a bad wife and mother because I'm a serious painter."

"You're not serious enough, my darling, because you don't know yourself."

"You're not an artist, mother. You can't judge – "

"I can't judge *you?*"

"No."

"Such conceit!"

"No! Defense!" shouted Barbara Stone, but her mental sword was obsolete against the affectionate amusement that had replaced her mother's usual anger.

"You don't accept who I am."

"A terrified child woke me up. I saw teeth marks in her flesh."

"We must have been playing one of the old games."

"You really don't remember?"

"It's not important."

"Not important?"

"Memory is selective, you know. Evidently, last night's occurrence meant nothing to me."

"It's terrific – I must finally tell you, I …"

"What?"

"Your confidence. Really!"

Suddenly replacing decades of hostility with approbation, Helen Reed waved away her daughter's suspicious response. Her fury, constantly shouted against Christy's masculine education, had affected Barbara Stone's conviction like wind against rock. Where had this great aplomb come from, and as Christy grew complex, why had it never faltered?

"I've always known exactly who Christy is. In the labor room, the baby's bloody head had a look of elegant marble. I welcomed her like a tiny warrior."

"Your warrior is my Victorian girl."

"No, mother."

"Can you be so sure?" Mrs. Reed implored with a shrug and charming smile.

"Yes! Just yes!"

"How?"

"I'm an artist, I tell you."

It was no effort for Helen Reed to smile and kiss her fingertips at her daughter. A real danger to Christy, this rabid arrogance completely justified her decision to create independence for the child with her wealth.

"I'd buy this drawing if I saw it in a gallery. What are you up to *now?*" Helen Reed clapped her hands as she looked at the pad. "It's my jacket on the back of this old iron chair. It looks as though I'm just out of sight – in my house or garden. It could be a picture of my death. How cordial, darling, how loyal."

"You don't like meaning, remember?"

"What meaning are you talking about? My jacket on the back of the chair is just what it is, and I want it tacked up over my bed. David knows where to buy thumbtacks if there are none in the kitchen drawer. What are you so pleased about?"

"You see that I love you and that I'm loyal?"

"Plain as day."

"I'm so glad," breathed her daughter.

"You can waste emotion on the normal in heat like this?"

"All winter I've been trying to paint your beautiful face from a photograph and I made you look awful."

"If you can't do portraits – don't. I tell you, darling, you can finally begin to make some money."

"Oh, Jake does that."

"Well, aren't you the lucky one?"

"Jake satisfies himself not me. I don't need a fancy apartment to paint in. I could paint anywhere."

"You couldn't paint if you were hungry and cold."

"Slightly hungry, slightly cold – I'd still be painting. Certainly, I don't need all this."

The dismissive sweep of her beloved estate by her daughter's sooty hand would have been, but for the planned change of her will, a perfect torment to Helen Reed. Her disgust at the heretical excess of her daughter's philosophy became gracious toleration. She praised her, smiling.

"You *could* live in a slum and paint. That wrecked dust pile you keep for your husband and child – you *do!*" She reached for her daughter's hand. "You're an eyesore for a lawyer's wife, but as yourself you're attractive, intelligent and fit. In circles where creativity is valued, well then, I even approve of your hair."

"My hair?"

"You look like an artist. A hot one, you crazy child! You draw my beautiful pool with your hair full of sweat and you don't go swimming!"

"I *will* swim!"

"I'll watch you."

Barbara Stone stepped onto the diving board and waved at the formal figure stained yellow by the umbrella's light. As she bounced high to imitate Christy's cocky front flip, she felt her feeling of shameful and clumsy exposure change to joy in the rays of her mother's gaze.

Clutching the edge of the pool as she struggled for breath, she looked up at her mother, casually held in David Sweeney's arms.

"Dear god, David, she landed on her back ..."

"She'll get it with practice."

"Tell her to kill herself, why don't you?" Helen Reed

feebly smiled at her daughter as her masseur carried her to the house. "Don't over do it, darling, just swim."

"I will," murmured Barbara Stone. "I'll obey my mother."

A jeering voice in her mind mocked her serenity as she thrust herself onto the pool's edge and dangled her legs in the water. The Weston house was a reflection on the gay, bobbing surface, the border of the pool, like a picture's frame, imparting the magic of containment.

"I grew up in paradise!"

This thought, ignoring the derision of her bitter, mental voice, grew radiant and Barbara Stone felt the mighty presence of her mother and father in the watery scene. Once, when the world was young, she'd won the approval of gods. A child's chest would be too narrow for the happiness she was feeling, as pressing her heart, she remembered a favorite dress from the glowing times, a sun dress, white with red polka dots and a belt. Polka dots flying, white shoes and socks, dying of love – she been her parents' darling.

Just then, David Sweeney opened the kitchen's screen door and stepped back onto the terrace. He walked to the table that was shaded by the yellow umbrella.

"Your mother wants this." He picked up the drawing pad and smiled at Barbara Stone as she lifted her eyes from his shimmering image and looked at him directly.

"I'm ordered to town to buy thumb tacks."

"Wait for me!"

In the bath house, her clothes were so resistant to her exuberance that she sat in the car with her sleeves ripped at the armpits and two buttons torn from the front of her shirt. David's long hair, streaming out the driver's window, appeared to salute her joy.

8

"I could be some damned burglar." The screen door shutting behind him, Jake spoke softly in the Weston house. The slammed taxi door at the front gate and his steps on the slate walk were the signals that every year had roused Helen Reed from her chair on the porch and propelled her to the front hall to proclaim that with his arrival, the fourth of July weekend had officially begun.

Exploring the empty downstairs, Jake pined for the cordial greeting. On the back porch, he discovered the yard's unholy accommodation of the widow's swimming pool. His hands were jabbing daggers in his pockets, as his eyes could find no spot where a tennis court wouldn't perpetuate the market decline of the Weston estate.

Shading his eyes from the morning sun, pitched forward on a muscular leg, Jake hunted for the masseur in the large yard. His conviction that a scoundrel would never exert himself with clippers or mow the grass in hot weather made the assiduously groomed garden an insult to his judgment.

He sneered at the freshly-edged flowerbed and the kitchen's shining order. The glass door of the tall pantry cupboards had been washed, showing sparkling china and crystal. Scoured pots and pans hung over the stove, along with a rack of gleaming, sharp knives. Bookcases, tables, even the personal drawers of Helen Reed's desk displayed to Jake's hostile scrutiny the vigorous order of an optimistic mind.

"Is that Christy drumming?" Jake asked himself on his way upstairs to find Helen Reed. He stopped and consciously acknowledged the drumming which, since putting down his suitcase, was accosting his ears. Her increased finesse, her talent and her will to attain perfection reminded the lawyer that the period beyond Helen Reed's dying, and fueled by her fortune, was likely to be the most vigorous of Christy's life.

"Ah, Jake, our famous weekend can begin."

"Helen?"

Propped on pillows, the sick woman closed her eyes to shut out the sight of her son-in-law's fright. "You can't help it, darling! I'm a gray, shriveled little thing."

"You're beautiful."

"That's what David Sweeney says – but I believe *him.*"

"You don't believe me?"

The voice and hair of his mother-in-law sprang from the fragile head with their old vigor and encouraged him to take her hand.

"You've got a grip like my husband," she smiled, loathing his peremptory strength.

As Jake stroked her arm she remembered the frustration and rage of her lonely arousal when Tom Reed rode his damned horse race between her legs. Ye gods, how she'd loathed the narcissistic rider.

"You remind Hal Busby of his old partner, too. Oh, yes! Over the years he's often said so."

"Then they must have battled."

"You've arrived if you're fighting with Hal Busby." Smiling at his excitement, she asked what the fight with the partner was about.

"I oppose the way Hal Busby is running the firm these days. He must expect me to be leaving."

"You concentrate on Hal Busby and set him straight. Don't bog down in worry. You'll have plenty of money when you win."

"If I win, Helen."

"Oh, words!"

The weary lift of her chin banished the dread of poverty from the lawyer's heart. Being sane she could not assume his victory over the tough senior partner. Obviously she was alluding to her death, when the family would be safe in her fortune.

"Are you in pain?"

"You know – my back." She turned on her side. "Go swimming."

"Your back?" Jake stared purposefully at the jutting spine. "Let's help you, Helen."

Doing the dog's breath – David had taught her – for

control in nature's grip, the widow shrieked at the fiery pain produced by his heavy fingers.

"I'm looking for your pills." Jake's voice trembled as he searched the bedside table. "I'll find them."

"No pills."

"What?"

"I need David."

"For god's sake – where is he?" The widow's suffering threw Jake into a panic and he strode, shouting, to the window. "Where the hell is he? You pay him enough to be useful – the *scoundrel!*"

When the pain receded Helen Reed regarded her son-in-law in tired triumph. There stood a hypocrite, converting his fright of physical agony into hostility as if, at his will, he could turn her against David Sweeney.

"He went for thumb tacks. Barbara, too."

"Thumb tacks?" A horrid nakedness as the sick woman struggled to sit up against the pillows kept Jake at the window.

"He should be shot."

"I sent him."

"He knows you have these pains."

"Would you have him stand at this bedside twenty-four hours a day?"

"You pay him enough, Helen."

"I'm not nearly rich enough to afford the value of David Sweeney's presence. My only hope is to attract him with pleasure. He tells me he's fond of a game of tennis

– now, wait, Jake." Secretly, she relished his heavy winded consternation. "I'm not in the mood for your 'hard time' lecture. I want enthusiasm."

"Well, my friend, of course you do. You've got a brand new swimming pool in your back yard and it's lonely."

"It's a miracle I've got Mr. Salvadore coming tomorrow – one of his big jobs was cancelled. His crew and a steam shovel will arrive at the crack of dawn. When I told him that I wanted to watch a tennis game on my own court before I died, he laughed so nicely and promised me he'd put his best person on the job. Oh, Jake, I'm so glad you say the pool is calling for a tennis court. It's lovely to be supported, don't you know?"

"I have no intention of giving you support. Oh, Christ, Helen, it's a terrible plan."

"Oh, but Jake! Think how peaceful it would be to play right here this weekend. No traffic to fight. Just kick off your sweaty gear and swim on the spot. Think of the time saved for your reading. Everyday that boy tells me how much he loves living here."

"A swimming pool, now a tennis court. Jesus, my beads, he's a pig in clover."

"He admires my old piano and writes the most beautiful songs."

"About what?"

"The migration of my soul."

"You don't believe in that nonsense."

He returned to the subject at hand. "The use of the

court will be too brief to justify the devaluation of your property."

"Speak English, please, as Christy says."

"Too much money, Helen, for too little time."

"Thank god for David Sweeney – whom I met in time."

"In time for what?"

"Pleasure."

"Whose pleasure?" Jake bristled. "Not yours, I think. Has your young man expressed a desire to learn tennis?"

"Oh, he's a very good player."

"Well, I think he can go and play on a town court, don't you?"

Such condescension from her father and husband had caused her to tremble and blush, but now with a rueful smile at Jake, she relished the arrival of rage.

"If David went swimming in the town pool I wouldn't have the pleasure of watching him."

"He's a scoundrel," Jake growled.

"Why? Because he's beautiful?"

"What's a young man doing being a masseur?"

"David Sweeney's a healer. I feel better every day."

"Oh, Helen."

"I know I'm dying," she looked steadily into his disgusted eyes.

"I'm only telling you that I feel happier as the days go on."

"He's a scoundrel."

"For making me happy?"

"For taking the credit."

"Well, naturally, a hardboiled Yankee can't embrace Eastern philosophy at my age, but I'm touched that David believes in my immortality. He's loyal, you see."

"Look here, Helen! Nature has no need to preserve a particular being beyond its particular span of life. Now, I'm dammed if reality makes me disloyal to you."

"You're speaking about your reality, my darling." Her unique endearment disguised his danger. "When I look into David Sweeney's eyes I feel protected by his belief. Cherished."

"Is eternity the mind of a masseur?"

"I'm being eaten alive, my dear – my poor, sad carcass. I'm glad the boy believes I have a soul. He comforts me."

Jake sat on the bed and gently embraced her. He endured her cool flaccidity and suspicious smell for ten beats of his racing heart then went back to the window.

"Helen, my friend," his breath burst from his lungs. "Our memories of all the wonderful things you've said and done. All our conversations about you, all our tears and laughter – this is your immortality."

"Oh, I'm sure my ears will be burning – but I won't have ears. I'll be a stinking mess in a steel box in the Weston Cemetery."

"You'll be in the hearts of your family."

"Bless your lawyer's mind," purred the widow while inwardly avid for his upset, "I've been thinking like a fool."

115

"He's been working on you."

"I shouldn't trust my feeling that he loves me and finds me beautiful?" Helen Reed answered his look of embarrassment with a melancholy smile. "If I wet myself at night, David just sweeps me up as though he were happy to see me."

"The fellow's outrageous."

"He totes me around the yard and every spot I pick is the perfect place for the tennis court to be built."

"A tennis court is an indulgence! You can't turn your estate into a white elephant for a month or two of enjoyment."

"That's eternity."

"Sixty odd days?"

"I'm doused in seconds when David touches me. I'm at a party, my dear." She despised Jake's dogged disapproval. "And I don't give a damn about a few thousand dollars more or less when this property is finally sold."

"Oh, Helen! Old friend!"

"I'm not a tragedy, Jake."

"You've lost your perspective because you're sick."

"Good riddance, I say."

"Good riddance to Helen Reed?" Jake was sincerely sad. "Your good sense, your graciousness and beauty are revered at the firm."

"What cancer has ever been more graciously received? As for my good sense, could any disease be better battled? Oh, smile, Jake. That lad's marvelous effect on me contradicts your worldly wisdom."

"He's pretending."

"David always stops the dreadful chewing."

"You're giving him the power."

"I know his hands like what they touch."

"Oh, Helen, isolated here, you've been overwhelmed."

Could he be right, her tough, confident son-in-law? Her faith faltering, Helen Reed suffered her back pain and the disobedience of Christy's constant drumming.

"Yank your daughter out of the cellar and take her for a swim. Then rest, Jake. You look exhausted."

"You're in pain again? Let's help you, Helen."

"Get David."

"Honest love will heal you." Jake rushed the widow onto her stomach. "Feel the difference." Her protesting groans announced an awful defeat, so Jake attacked the old woman's spine with unconscious aggression. Sliding his persecuting thumbs from her neck to her coccyx, he commanded her tears to stop and her mind to help him.

"Stop!"

"Don't cry! Focus! It's on the run. Kick it out, Helen! There! There! There! Take the pain, darling! Use it against the parasite. Use it! Use it! Damn!"

Turning the weeping widow onto her back, he regretted her failure to galvanize her will. "The thing was receding, darling, but you didn't have the stuff."

Helen Reed looked up at his hectoring finger and hated the triggered memory of her husband. His penis impatiently tugged from between her legs and her frigidity mocked as though with queenly calm she'd declined to flick the switch of her desire.

"The weaker I get the more you remind me of Tom Reed. You're the warrior of this family." She gasped with pain and anger. "The car's back."

Jake returned to the window and observed David Sweeney in the driveway with menacing rectitude.

"Oh, Christ, look at the hair!" He passed his hand over his own dark, cropped head.

"Please go down and tell David to bring up the thumb tacks. Be polite," she cajoled her son-in-law, the advancing destruction of his life as evident to her eyes as his suave pride. "I want him to pin up Barbara's drawing before he begins the birthday cooking."

"I'm always polite to your servants, my dear." Tipping her a merry nod, Jake went whistling down the stairs.

9

Helen Reed drank her noon martinis from a silver thermos that her darling boy had left at her bedside. His indignation when she'd told him of Jake's coarse handling, and his fear that she would be lonely while he served the family lunch at the pool made their sounds through her window the stimulus of a sensual revenge.

Sipping icy cocktails with closing eyes, she passionately visualized the canvas chairs that David Sweeney had purchased and set up at the pool for the comfort of her daughter and son-in-law. The chairs, in her reveling, became a prelude to improvements – the enchanted domesticity of her valiant old house. At the same time, as plain old real estate, its compromised market value would be poison in Jake Stone's veins.

Beneath the dowager's window and the blazing noon sun, David Sweeney, presenting a tray of sandwiches to Lawyer Stone, heard the diving board and exploding water as Christy, relentlessly diving, pursued her mastery of the double front flip.

Twin canvas chairs placed side by side held the accomplished parents. The mother drawing, the father with a book.

"She did it, Mr. Stone."

"One summersault or two."

"I saw two, sir."

David put down the tray and his arms shot up in silent salute. He walked along the pool ready to pull her out, but she frowned and swam away from his hand.

"Smile, honey, I know you're proud."

"Shut up," she whispered, her strong arms hauling her body from the water. "Go away!"

Her acute embarrassment engendered his own. As she lay down on her stomach between her parents, he grabbed the long pole of the skimmer and began clearing drowned beetles from the sparkling water.

Lawyer Stone commanded his daughter. The knowledge of his insight, announced to Helen Reed, was wan comfort, as David obeyed the newcomer's stern will. He felt that the hour that separated his last friendly conversation with Barbara Stone from this servile silence was now an invisible barrier to congenial return.

In the car, Barbara's account of her mother's sudden respect had been so moving. Helen Reed liked the drawing of her jacket and didn't he agree that the thumbtacks to be bought must be red white and blue? He loved her bursting copper hair the way he loved nature and when she took the tacks to the cashier it was like a tree paying leaves. By her side, driving back and forth from town, he'd felt happy and at ease. But now, stinking to high heaven in the mind of this aristocrat – oh woe – he was afraid.

"Good god, Bobbie," her husband growled as she sketched David Sweeney. "Are you recording the last days of an endangered species?"

"A unique species, pal, and I've never drawn better."

"Says who?"

"My mother."

"You hate Helen's taste in art."

"Have you seen my other drawing on the wall by her bed?"

Jake Stone shook his finger. "Magazine junk, Barbara. What's the matter with you?"

"I've gotten what I've always wanted."

"A gold star for your drawing of a tennis court? You'll die happy? I've seen the damage, on your mother's wall – to the yard – to us!"

"If the last project of mother's life makes this house a white elephant, our family will survive."

"How many times this winter have you heard the news that I'm going to be a partner without pay?"

"So, be an Abogado. I love your story about the cheerful Hispanic man. One of the struggling tens of thousands. Oh, why not? I could do portraits in the park or paint apartments. Leave shining walls in my wake – we could meet for beers in our neighborhood bar."

Jake Stone sat up and hit the back of the drawing pad.

At the loud rap and her mother's yell, Christy, still sunning herself between her parents, flung a towel over her head.

"The women of this family are a pack of infatuated fools."

"You say that about our daughter?"

Under the towel, Christy winced in her mother's protective grip.

"Weren't we both watching Christy dive?" said Jake.

"I certainly was."

"Did you see a woman? No, absolutely not!" Jake drowned out his wife's protests. "Christy promised me she'd slim down and I'm delighted to see her looking so fit." He leaned and briskly smacked her rump. "Good girl, I'm delighted with you."

The upward sweep of blood from her body burned Christy's face. Her butt was still jiggling from her father's rap when she felt her bathing suit plucked back.

"What's this?" Barbara Stone touched the tooth marks that several nights ago in seething drunkenness she'd left on her daughter's buttocks. Her husband's shocked whistle acknowledged the mean bruise.

"What is it?"

"Sex," Barbara Stone robustly declared. "Our daughter's having sex."

"Stop your silly stuff!"

"Hats off to the sexual revolution," cried Barbara Stone with mournful vigor. "Hats off to where it's at!"

"The child hurt herself diving, Barbara. Don't lose your head."

Hating Christy's confident parents, David Sweeney flung down the skimmer.

"Ask her!" he shouted. Gripping the backs of their chairs, he stared down at Christy's towel covered head and shivering body.

"Your parents are talking for you. Are you some dog lying here? Should I tell the truth for you?"

"What's the truth?" asked Barbara Stone, dread slowing her heart. Her husband's fierce grip hurt her arm.

"Come on now, darling, we ask him for dessert, not the truth."

"He knows, Jake."

"Who knows? Who is this stranger?"

"He loves mother and Christy and he knows about me." Alarmed at her misery, Jake put his hand over her fingers, which covered the nasty bruise.

"What are you saying?"

"I bit the hell out of Christy, I really hurt her."

Good and bad, marriage had displayed many states to David Sweeney, but never this lawyer's emotional chivalry that would rescue his lady from truth's increasing distress.

Jake Stone shot up from his chair as though to protect his wife from a mortal wound. He recounted how the crocodile chase had been one of Christy's favorite childhood games.

He remembered a wee gal demanding, until she'd

dropped, the repetition of scary excitement. Learning courage and the pleasure of fear, Christy had been trained to succeed in the violence of masculine competition. Playfully, patiently, Barbara Stone had brought up a crackerjack kid!

"A jealous, drunken woman attacked our daughter. ME!"

"Absolutely not!"

"Yes!"

"When you have one too many you become a different person. A person you never remember in the morning."

"It isn't an excuse – that I don't remember."

"What should you remember, a creature made from booze and fatigue?" He kissed her woeful mouth. "Start counting your drinks, if you like, but don't reproach yourself."

"You *must* understand," she agonized. "Every night I turn myself into a hideous reptile. Instead of your 'good mother,' I'm Christy's nightmare."

Her husband's handsome confidence, one hand on his jutting hip, the other in graceful gesture, was a stifling enemy. Leaning in her chair, Barbara Stone looked past his granite body to see the glowing, young man.

"David Sweeney knows I can't take care of our daughter. He does!"

The lawyer's hips creaked in his calm study of the boy. "A masseur?"

"He's a musician!" Throwing off the towel, Christy

rushed to David and tried to look into his averted eyes.

"Tell dad about your hit song. What's wrong?" she cried at his weird, scared face.

"I know how he sees me."

"You've recorded four albums. Tell him!"

Hurrying to the house, David's handsome authenticity appeared to be dissolving.

"What's wrong with him?"

Christy lay down again between the two new canvas chairs where her parents lay back. She shivered from her mother's gentle fingers on her bruise and the flow of her father's exciting but foreign sounding words.

"I've been reading about the cancer-causing virus, and it strikes me that the character of Helen's masseur is being revealed to me – symbolically, of course."

"Speak English, man!"

"If Christy doesn't understand what I am saying, well then, her weak vocabulary will doom her to a third rate life!"

"I'm sorry, darling." Her mother's whisper came again and again beneath her father's loud college lecture. Barbara Stone was sorry about the jealousy, sorry to be the crocodile, sorry, sorry, sorry to be hurting her.

Jake Stone was fascinated to learn that a virus led the life of a parasite. It was a packet of wandering genes on the lookout for a cell that it could board and loot for its own prosperity.

"Hey, Christy? Sound like anyone you know?"

10

"My shot!"

David Sweeney turned his fearful eyes away from Helen Reed and explored the objects of the bedroom that were prettily receiving the strong rays of the afternoon sun. Shining wood, glass that sparkled. The white cotton of the pillow beneath his friend's restless head was in savage glow.

"The light's pouring in here! It's time for your massage, not your shot."

"I need it!"

Spread over the pillow, the gray waves of her hair seemed in flight from her suffering face, and when David lifted her, she panted and wept.

"Jake woke up the pain – his imperious fingers. Oh, please, don't put me down."

"I don't believe he touched you."

David carried her to the window and supported her trembling head as she looked down into the yard.

"I can still feel his revulsion – oh, the hypocrite – thinking that his honest love was shaming yours. Look at him now, reading away in my garden with his back to my beautiful house. He's so sure he's won the future."

"The lawyer worked on your back! But, why?"

"To expose my darling boy as a fortune hunter. Oh, but hasn't he only exposed himself?" Her rabid triumph repelled David Sweeney and rocking her, he prepared to argue for her better mind.

"I'm in agony from *his* hands – so stiff and remote – not yours. I remembered how hating my husband was a terrible burden, because I was timid. You must be encouraged ..."

"No!" David Sweeney was revolted. "I'll always feel like a servant when Lawyer Stone's about."

"You'll get braver."

"I know I won't."

"When you're the steward here – "

"He's too strong for me."

"Nonsense."

David held her head steady and commanded her to look at the truth of the poolside scene below her eyes. The calm, occupied parents on the canvas chairs, the child between them – she must get the picture!

"Christy lay with that towel over her head while her father insulted me."

"Ah, but she's a child."

"I don't blame her, don't think that. I just understand that she is totally loyal to her parents."

128

"To me she's loyal!"

The sudden strength of her wasted arms had David struggling to hold her. His eyes watered from the sharp twist of her hands in his hair and, as she commanded, he looked down into the yard and saw Christy pulling on the arms of her parent's chairs to get onto her feet.

"She's had her little rest and she's coming inside," she observed. "They're not even looking up from their books and pads – not a glance after her. Bad parents both!"

Head down, Christy walked into the house. Quickly, drumbeats followed the pace of her resolute step.

"Oh, no! Don't I hear a victory march?" cried Helen. "It's coming up as though the house were a megaphone. Lost in his useless book, Jake Stone doesn't hear it, but I can feel the house marching down on him. Oh, my chest is banging!"

Alarmed, David put her down on the bed.

"Tomorrow Mr. Salvadore is coming with his crew and I'm going to see you smash Jake Stone on my new tennis court. Oh, god, the drumming is so strong! It's hurting me! Stop her! Stop the child!"

David watched her banging heart with dread.

"I can't leave you now."

"Stop Christy before she kills me!"

His hand skimming the banisters, the masseur dropped down to the coal bin in giant bounds.

"Stop!" he yelled, then grabbed her sticks. Chagrined by her sorrowful rage, he pleaded.

"Go upstairs to your grandmother now!"

"My father thinks you're sleaze."

"Hurry!"

He ran to the door and ran back as she ignored his desperate summons.

"You didn't fight him."

"I'm sorry."

"WHY?" She grabbed back the drumsticks.

"Helen's dying!" He beckoned violently as he bolted for the stairs.

"Hurry!"

"I hate you."

The girl's furious drumming pursued him up the stairs, and continued as he sank down beside Helen Reed and held her while her heart pounded.

He lied, telling her that Christy was drumming her way around the furniture downstairs, playing exuberant tribute to her grandmother captive in the bed; beating rhythms on her favorite furniture.

His words produced no effect, however; the widow was in another place.

"Helen, look up here at your daughter's drawing!"

Turning her head with gentle hands, David directed the widow's gaze to the sketch of her jacket cordially hanging on the back of an iron chair.

"Bobbie," the widow gasped and saw in a flash that a mind, milling with memories and impetuous feelings, thoughts and scenes, was eternity, not apart from the rushing of breath and blood.

Helen Reed was about to refute the lad's dreary abstraction when her chest struck a terrific blow.

David bent over her, weeping. In convulsive agony, as her heart stopped beating, Helen Reed plunged her hands into the masseur's thick, glossy hair. She was leaving eternity. Leaving, leaving!

"God loves you," David promised his horrified friend. "Believe me!"

– FIN –

About the Author

Joan Hawkins was born in Cambridge, Massachusetts. She attended Bennington College and New York University. She has lived most of her life in Manhattan, practicing psychotherapy there. Her debut novel, *Underwater*, was published by GP Putnam in 1974. The book was critically acclaimed, challenging traditional gender roles and exploring controversial issues of the day. A second edition of *Underwater* was published on its fortieth anniversary by Landon Books in 2014.

Joan's second novel, *Bailey* (2012), explores themes of addiction and childhood trauma. *Rematch* (2021), her fourth book, is a prescient take on corporate sexual discrimination set in the early eighties. Joan's fifth work, *Family Money*, was published by 451 Editions in 2022 along with the electronic edition of *Underwater*. *Trespass* is the author's third novel.

For more, see: www.JoanHawkins.net

Landon Books, NEW YORK